Contents

JULIA JARRETT

Protecting Anna

A Lucky Strike Lovers Novel

First edition

ISBN: 978-1-7771324-4-6

Editing by Aimee Walker
Cover art by J.M. Walker

This book was professionally typeset on Reedsy.
Find out more at reedsy.com

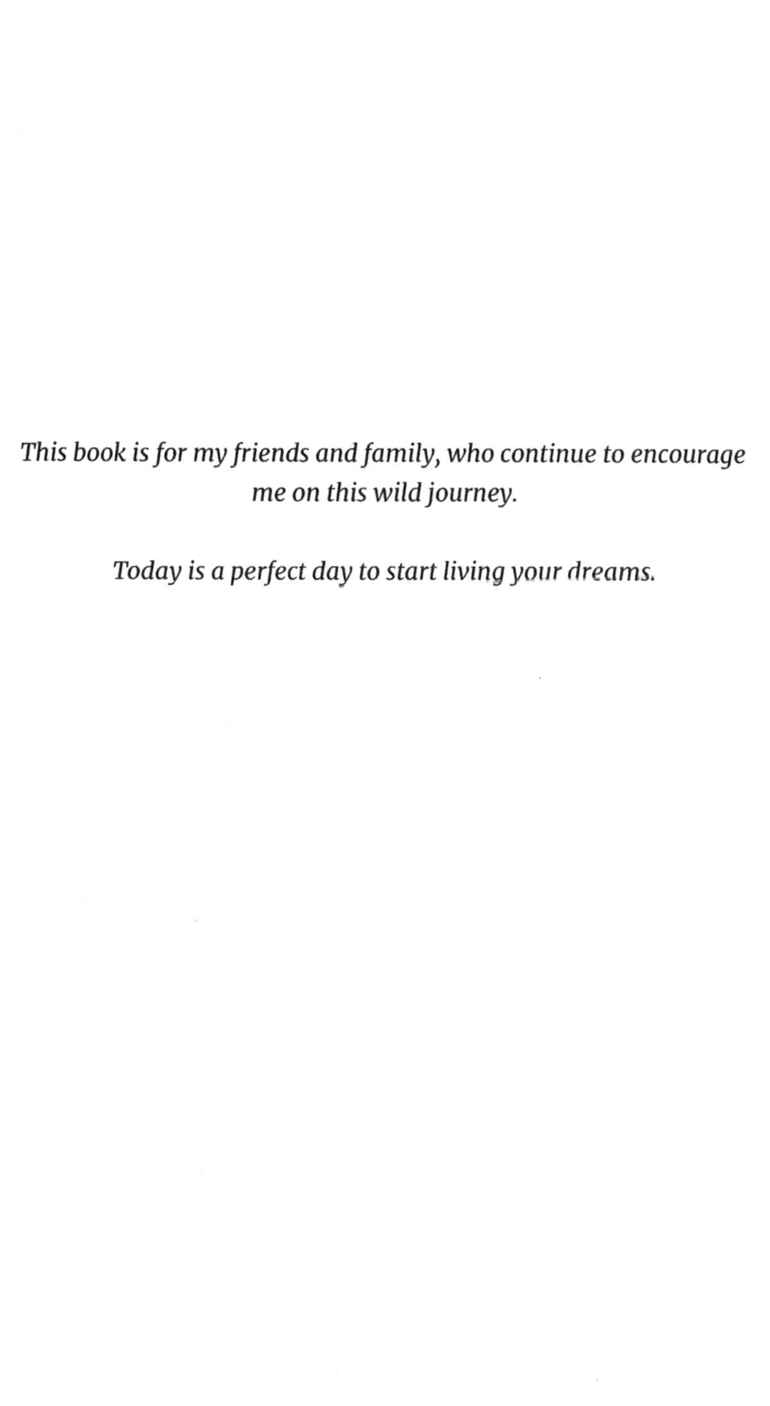

This book is for my friends and family, who continue to encourage me on this wild journey.

Today is a perfect day to start living your dreams.

Preface

Protecting Anna is book two of The Lucky Strike Lovers Quartet.

If you have not read book one, Loving Callie, I suggest you do that first - although it is not necessary as Protecting Anna can be enjoyed as a stand-alone novel.

Loving Callie is available on Amazon now.

WARNING: This story alludes to abusive and toxic relationships. If this is a trigger for you, please proceed with caution. There is a guaranteed HEA and no overtly descriptive scenes of abuse.

1

Prologue

Thirteen hours on a bus is a long time with nowhere to go and nothing to do except lose oneself in the murky depths of one's thoughts. For Anna Thorn, the thirteen hours she sat on the bus taking her from Sacramento to Portland were spent alternating between regret over how her life had turned out over the past two years, horror from her memories of two nights ago, and hope that she could somehow move on from it all.

She had never imagined that she could fall prey to an abuser. Surely, she was smarter than that, but it was that kind of naïve thinking that led to Anna's downfall. Even intelligent and educated women could be manipulated by men who used fear and control to prey on women. Over the two years that she was with her ex, Tim Fox, she had slowly lost everything and everyone that mattered to her, until she was nothing more than a puppet on his string.

In the beginning, Tim was the consummate boyfriend. Kind, generous, and affectionate. He overwhelmed her with grand gestures, and constant attention. So what, if he was jealous of the time she spent on campus at class or hanging out with her college friends, surely that just meant he missed her. His insistence that she move in with him after only a few months together was sweet, wasn't it? When he would comment that she 'owed him' for the gifts he gave, she readily agreed. He was her boyfriend after all, and shouldn't relationships be a give and take? It didn't seem to matter that he would always take much more than he would give. That foolishly blind attitude was how Anna ended up trapped in the dark depths of Tim's control, much as a fly could be caught in a spider's web.

It was when he started to push her to drop out of school, promising to support her and telling her she didn't need a degree or a job if she was with him, that Anna first started to wonder about his intentions. When they first met, he had seemed so supportive of her dream to become a kindergarten teacher. Still, she gave in to his insistence that she stay home, she was so caught up in the fantasy he had spun of a happy life together. Surely once they were married and had children, he would let her complete her education.

A short while after she left school, Tim started to change. Instead of seemingly harmless comments, he began to exert his control in more frightening ways, tightening his hold on Anna. First, he sold her car without telling her. Then he sent a letter of resignation to her boss at the coffee shop she worked at part-time, essentially stranding her at his apartment in Sacramento. His displeasure any time Anna tried to make plans to see her friends grew and grew, to the point that she didn't want to upset him and simply stopped trying. When he gave her a new phone, complete with a new number, he *accidentally* erased her contact list making it impossible for her to reach anyone. Anytime Anna would try to talk to him, to confront him about his actions, he would morph back into the loving man she had first fallen for. He would insist that all they needed was each other and that he would provide for her. And so, the cycle would repeat. Tim would be sneakily manipulative and controlling, Anna would try to stand up for herself, Tim would smother her with attention and cause her to feel so much guilt that she would let her concerns slide.

Over time, his demeanor began to change. Instead of attempting to maintain a facade of affection, he allowed his true nature to be revealed—cold and cruel. Where his manipulations had always been couched in false platitudes of love, now he was more blatant with his arrogant and heartless desire to control Anna. She gradually became fearful of his reaction if she were to push back, and so her protests died away. The rational voice inside of her knew, it was only a matter of time before his emotional torment of her turned physical. His insidious comments and threats had done their job; they acted like drips of water carving out stone over time, eating away at Anna's confidence—eventually leaving her a shell of a woman who was too mortified and too terrified of his reaction to ever reach out for help. By the time she realized that his endless supply of money was because he was a high-level dealer who provided illicit drugs to many of California's notorious gangs, it was too late for her to back out of the relationship safely, or so Tim led her to believe.

In the end, it was a letter from a lawyer in Portland Oregon that was the catalyst to Anna taking control of her life again. The day the letter arrived was the first time in a long time that luck seemed to be on her side. Tim had tossed the mail on the counter as he barked orders at someone on the phone. Out of the corner of her eye, Anna happened to notice the Portland return address, and curiosity had her stealthily looking at the envelope. When she discovered her name in the address line, she had snuck the letter into her pocket and that night she began to plan her escape. However, despite her attempts to hide everything from Tim, Anna knew he must have suspected something had changed. He became obsessed with never letting her out of sight, and, if he had to leave the apartment without her, he began to lock the front door from the outside. The unending fear she felt at being completely at his mercy was consuming. This man owned her, body and soul. Still, Anna prayed desperately that she would get an opportunity to run.

His preoccupation with keeping her close, was what led to the events that haunted her. Anna found herself sitting in the front seat of his car one night, while he went to one of his *work meetings*. She had been scared before but nothing like what she had felt that night. She knew her life was in danger and terror ran through her veins.

Even now, hundreds of miles away from where it took place, sitting on a bus that raced her away from him, she could see the events take place in her mind as clear as ever.

Feeling too anxious and filled with dread to sit still, Anna had fidgeted with her hands as she waited for Tim. Through the tinted back window, she saw another vehicle pull up and a man step out. Tim approached him and they talked for a minute. What happened next all occurred so quickly it was as if it were a nightmare playing out in front of her at warp speed. A nightmare she would never forget. When it was over, Tim had made a brief phone call, then came back to the car without a word and drove them home. He dropped Anna off, locking her inside as usual, then headed off to god only knows where, leaving her trembling with fear.

Later, when she thought about what she had done, Anna

would wonder if an angel had directed her actions. Why else would she have thought to take out her phone and record what had played out right in front of her eyes?

The next two days were fraught with tension. Tim was rarely at the apartment and when he was, Anna could sometimes overhear frantic conversations on the phone. People would come to the apartment at all hours, why, she didn't know as Tim always shut her in the bedroom when they did. Still, it didn't take a genius to notice Tim's stress, or the fact that his clothing and computers seemed to disappear, coinciding with those late-night visitors. Was he preparing to leave? She had no idea, and that uncertainty fueled her desperate desire to get away.

Only once in those two days was Anna brave enough, or stupid enough, to say something to Tim. It had been a seemingly innocent question she thought, about where a particular sweater of hers was. For some reason that set him off into a blind rage and led to the one instance of him becoming physically violent to her. She had the bruises on her arms from when he grabbed her as a reminder of just how volatile the situation was.

The night that her prayers were answered was unlike any night before. Tim had never been one to sample his own wares, but that evening Anna knew he had taken a hit of something, she could see it in the glazed look in his eyes when he came into the bedroom looking for her. He gave her a once-over look of disdain, then fell onto the bed and passed out. She had not been worried about him trying to force her into sex for a while, she knew he had many other women he used for that. The way he would come home stinking of perfume and sex, with rumpled clothes and a cruelly arrogant smirk told her that she had no value to him in the bedroom. For that, she was eternally thankful.

That night, with Tim passed out on the bed, Anna quickly packed a bag with clothes and the few meaningful belongings she had left. A stack of cash on the counter went into her jacket pocket along with the SIM card that she popped out of the cell phone he had given her. She knew she should go straight to the police with the video, but right now her focus was solely on getting as far away from Tim and his network of control as possible, and that meant leaving California.

She knew that if Tim ever figured out that she knew what had happened, he would come after her. And so, she ran for her life. All she could do now was lay low and pray her past would never catch up.

2

Chapter 1

The Lucky Strike pub was uncharacteristically quiet, thanks to the snowstorm blowing outside. January was cold in Portland, so cold that most people were staying inside instead of venturing out to pubs and restaurants.

Ryan Carlisle leaned against the back wall behind the bar and crossed his arms. Not much to do as a bartender when there were only a couple of customers.

His best friend, and co-owner of the pub, Jake Evans, sighed in irritation. “This place is dead. Why the hell are we still here? I could be home with Callie right now, she’s on her days off, and I’m stuck in an empty bar,” he muttered. Jake’s new fiancée, Callie Scott, was an emergency room doctor at a local hospital. Her hectic schedule combined with the demand on his time at the pub meant they had precious little time together.

Ryan smiled sympathetically. “Damned if I know, man. That last group looks like they are almost ready to settle up. Why don’t you head out, and I’ll just close up early when they leave. I’ll get on social media now to let people know we’ll be closed.”

Ryan enjoyed his role as co-owner and head bartender, but

recently he had been trying to take over more of the administrative tasks to give Jake time to focus on his relationship. After all, it wasn't as if he had someone special to go home to each night.

"Thanks, that would be great," Jake replied with a grateful smile. He put away the cloth he had been using, untied his bar apron and headed toward the back to collect his coat and leave.

As Ryan stood alone behind the bar, he wondered if he would ever be ready for a relationship like Jake's. Going home to the same woman each night, sharing a home and a life with someone. It was not something he had ever envisioned for himself, but he had to admit, seeing the loving connection between Jake and Callie stirred up strange feelings of longing within him.

He was growing tired of the playboy-bachelor lifestyle he had been living since college, when a devastating knee injury ended his soccer scholarship and dreams of a career in the major leagues. These days, he found himself wanting to build a life in Portland that didn't only revolve around one-night stands, but perhaps included something more meaningful.

Even as this wistful thought crossed his mind, Ryan could feel his defensive inner walls go up. He had always believed that marriage and a family were not in the cards for him. Growing up he had been forced to watch his mom struggle every single day to keep their family together. His deadbeat dad had cheated on his mom over and over, before taking off for good when he was just a baby. Molly Carlisle had been left alone with the job of raising two boys, Ryan and his older brother, Noah. She had sacrificed everything to keep the boys happy, fed, and healthy.

Ryan had vowed early on in his adult life that he would never do that to a woman. He would never allow himself to be in a situation where he could possibly hurt someone the way his dad had hurt his mom. If there was one lesson he had learned from his father's actions, it was that love had the power to hurt. So, to avoid that risk, Ryan lived by the belief that it was better to just avoid love entirely.

His somber musings over his past were interrupted by a customer coming to ask for their bill. As he rung up the tab, comfortably chatting with the older gentleman about the extreme weather, the front door opened, bringing in a gust of cold air. Ryan looked up, curious and just a little annoyed that someone new might be delaying his journey home. At first glance all he could see was a slight figure, bundled in a thick jacket, hat, and scarf. But when the newcomer took off her hat, and unleashed a cascade of wavy, mahogany brown hair, Ryan's attention perked up. And when his curious gaze met the soft, hesitant look that glanced furtively around the bar, Ryan was struck by an intensely protective feeling in his gut, unlike anything he had ever experienced. He didn't know who this woman was, but he immediately wanted to fold her into his arms and promise to keep her safe. The intensity of this thought was quickly followed with a healthy dose of cynicism as he realized how insane it was to want to protect a complete stranger, but Ryan was intrigued to find out who she was, and why she was in his bar.

* * *

Anna took in a deep, fortifying breath before making her way to the front of the bar where an incredibly handsome man stood, watching her approach. She took in his light hair, day old scruff, and piercing blue eyes that seemed to see straight into her soul. He was temptation personified, but Anna knew she had to keep a low profile and figure her life out before she could consider allowing someone new into her life. It had been a long day traveling up from California, with the weather becoming wetter and colder the farther north she went.

Safe in her coat pocket was a house key for her Aunt Theresa's house, the same house Anna had grown up in before moving to California. It was a miracle that she still had the key to the house after all this time. Perhaps a small, hopeful part of her had known that someday she would return.

When Anna had left the Portland bus depot and entered the snowstorm, she knew she needed to find a warm place with a phone and something to eat. She had eaten the granola bars she had managed to sneak into her pack hours ago, and her stomach was growling. The closest establishment to the depot that appeared to be open was this pub, The Lucky Strike. The warm, inviting atmosphere, even with barely any patrons, was comforting in the face of her emotional and physical exhaustion. But that brief feeling of comfort turned into something inexplicable, when Anna laid eyes on the bartender. She felt herself instantly attracted to him, with an intensity she had never felt before. He was pure sex on two legs, and while a small part of her longed to feel what it would be like to be in his arms, safe and secure, the other part was terrified by her emotional reaction. The last time Anna had been this intensely drawn to someone was Tim, and that had turned into a nightmare.

* * *

Ryan was captivated by the beauty in front of him. Her nervousness was palpable as she approached the bar, and when she got close, he could see the exhaustion in her face. That didn't stop her from being the most beautiful woman he had ever seen. Long brown hair fell down her back in silky waves, her eyes were a curious shade that he couldn't quite make out in the dim light of the bar, but they seemed golden with flecks of green. Long lashes swept her cheeks, and the frame of her body was small, almost delicate with a hidden vulnerability. His desire to protect this woman, crazy as it seemed, only intensified as she got closer.

When she reached the bar and spoke, in a soft musical voice, Ryan felt it like a gut punch.

"I know it's kind of a weird thing to ask for in a bar, but do you have any coffee? I wasn't sure where else would be open." She looked up at his face briefly before returning her eyes down to her hands which were folded in her lap.

"Yeah, I've got coffee. Can I get you anything to eat?" Ryan was embarrassed by the rough tone in his voice and hoped the mystery woman couldn't tell how affected he was by her.

"Whatever is easy, thank you."

He nodded and headed into the kitchen to pour her a steaming cup of coffee. While he was there, he fired up the grill to make a quick sandwich. Grabbing the carton of cream out of the fridge and some sugar, he returned to the bar, half expecting her to be gone.

He was relieved to find she was still sitting there. When she reached for the mug, with a small smile of thanks, the sleeve of her sweater pulled back just enough to reveal some partially faded bruises that looked suspiciously like someone had grabbed her and pulled her arm. Ryan noticed, and while his heart pounded with fierce anger that anyone would dare physically hurt this—or any—woman, he knew in his gut that drawing attention to it would likely make her flee. So, he pretended not to see anything, and tried to engage her in some light conversation.

Over the next ten minutes, as she devoured the grilled cheese sandwich he brought her, Ryan learned Anna's name and that she had recently moved to Portland from California. When she dodged any questions about her life in California, he again pretended not to notice, recognizing that there was a lot she was not telling him. To try and make her more comfortable, Ryan regaled her with tales of renovating and opening the bar and shared some funny stories about some of the repeat customers. Slowly he could see her relax, as a smile came more easily to her face.

"So, Anna, if you're planning on staying in Portland, have you figured out a job or a place to stay?" Ryan asked innocently, hoping the personal question didn't spook her.

"Yeah, my aunt left me a house when she died. Finding a job might be a bit more difficult, I, ummm, haven't been working much the last couple of years." That was the first piece of somewhat personal information she had shared, and Ryan stowed it away in his mind carefully. Then he let out a small laugh, and adopted a teasing tone to reply, "Well if you have any experience waitressing or bartending, I'll hire you in a heartbeat. We're desperate to find someone to help out around here."

"I worked at a café in high school, and worked as a waitress for a bit during my first year of college. Does that count?"

"Consider yourself hired," Ryan answered with a wink and a grin. "Seriously, if you're interested, come on by tomorrow afternoon. The storm should have died down by then and you can meet my buddy, Jake, he actually owns the place, and we'll get you started." He quickly wrote his name and number on a piece of paper and pushed it over to Anna. "Give me a call if you need anything. And if you change your mind it's okay, no hard feelings. But Anna? I hope you come back."

Anna stood, pulling on her jacket. "Thank you, Ryan, I'll be here. Tonight has been more than I expected. Thanks for the coffee and the company." She hesitated, and a blush covered her cheeks. "I'm sorry to ask you to do more for me, but can I use your phone to call a cab? I don't have a cell phone."

The flash of fear on her face stirred up the protective instinct in Ryan and made it even more obvious that Anna's move to Portland had been a rushed decision. Ryan's suspicions that something bad had happened to her only grew.

"No cab is going to be driving safely in this weather. Give me ten minutes to lock up, and I'll drive you home okay? My truck has snow tires... and I promise I'm not a psycho," he said, with what he hoped was a charming and teasing grin, to try and ease any fears she might have about getting in a car with a stranger.

Anna looked up at him with a mixture of wonder and relief on her face, before nodding in agreement. "Thank you, Ryan, that would be wonderful. Can I help you close up? It seems the least I could do since you're giving me a ride and a job."

"Nah, I've got this. We didn't have many customers today so I can come in early tomorrow to finish most of it. Let me just put the dirty glasses in the dishwasher and turn it on. I'll get my truck warming up out back as well."

Ryan watched her sit back down at the bar and return to fidgeting with the edges of her coat. He was pleased to see she seemed much less nervous than when she had first arrived.

A slight thrill ran though his body at the realization that this woman trusted him with her safety. Ryan had never let a woman get this close to him, so close that he felt responsible for them. It was a heady feeling to realize he was not running away from the responsibility. No, for once, he wanted to run straight toward it, toward Anna.

3

Chapter 2

The drive home was surprisingly comfortable. The instinctual trust she felt around Ryan was surprising, but Anna was doing her best to accept it. However, her nerves held her back from speaking, so Ryan kept the conversation flowing, without her needing to contribute too much. Before she knew it, Anna was looking out the window at a house she hadn't seen in over two years.

Anna had always been close to her aunt, even more so after her parents died in a car accident when she was just a child. Aunt Theresa had raised her, in this very house. They had learned how to transition a friendly aunt–niece relationship into one where Anna respected Aunt Theresa in her role as guardian and caregiver. She had been there as Anna hit puberty, high school and all the corresponding drama, events that seemed so trivial now. Anna's heart broke at the thought that her beloved aunt had died without Anna even knowing she was sick.

When Tim had changed her phone, Aunt Theresa's number was the only one she could recall. He had allowed her to stay in contact, via phone calls, once a week, that he was always present for. In hindsight, Anna realized that was probably just so that her aunt didn't get suspicious of their relationship.

In her passing, Aunt Theresa had provided a way out of the hell Anna had found herself in. Her childhood home was now in her name with the mortgage paid off in full. It was more than she could have dreamed of, and one final, poignant reminder of how her aunt would always love her.

Tonight, the house stood tall and dark, without a porch light on. The snow had piled up in the drive and the path to the front door was hidden. Still, Anna felt the familiarity of home, and knew she could find her way. She just hoped that the power had not been shut off. She turned to Ryan. "Thank you for the ride, Ryan, it was more than I expected tonight. Honestly, everything you've said and done has made my night so much better than it could have been."

She held her breath as he reached out and gently tucked a piece of her hair behind her ears. He was looking right at her, but instead of fear, she felt peace from his touch.

"It's no trouble. I'm glad you came into my bar, and I'm grateful you trusted me enough to see you home safe." His voice rang with truth and strength, a strength Anna felt infusing her soul. "Everything is going to work out, Anna, you'll see. I'll make sure of it."

It could have sounded controlling, but it didn't. Anna believed that his intentions were pure, and this was a man who only wanted to help—not hurt her.

On impulse, Anna reached across the center console to give Ryan a hug. If he was surprised, he didn't show it, holding her securely but with a gentle touch. Pulling back after a moment, Anna immediately missed the feel of Ryan's strong arms embracing her. It had felt like heaven to be held by someone again.

"Well, I should get inside and make sure I can still turn the lights on." Anna hoped her light tone was enough to dispel the simmering heat she could sense starting to build from that innocent hug.

"I'll walk you to the door."

"No really, it's okay."

"Anna, I insist." The look of firm but kind resolve in Ryan's deep blue eyes was enough to get Anna to acquiesce.

In silence they trudged toward the house together, Ryan thoughtfully stomping down a path through the snow with his much larger feet. On the porch, Anna dug the key out of her pocket and opened the front door. She was deeply relieved when the lights came on. Turning back to Ryan, she found herself hesitating. Their brief embrace in his truck had lit a spark that she was both drawn to and scared of. Anna was filled with the fear that Tim would somehow find her and tear her away from any sort of life she built. She knew there was no way she could start a relationship of any kind other than friendship. Still, she felt a pang of regret that Tim had the power to ruin something before it could truly begin. Not that she could define what that thing was, she just knew the feelings between her and Ryan could lead to something amazing, if her life were not such a mess. She straightened her spine, and felt her resolve stiffen with it. She stuck her hand out awkwardly for a handshake, to avoid another tempting hug. "Well, I guess I'll see you tomorrow afternoon. Thanks again for everything, Ryan."

He glanced down at her hand, then back at her quizzically, then took her hand and held it warmly. "I'll be here to drive you to the bar around noon, okay?"

She struggled to ignore the warmth that filled her heart at his selfless offer. So much for keeping her distance, this man was making it impossible for her to stay away. "Oh, you don't have to, really, I can walk or take the bus. I can't keep imposing."

"Anna, hear me please, I just want to help. My mom raised me to care for others and help if I can. Giving you a ride is no big deal, so please let me." His voice rang with sincerity, and Anna could do nothing more than nod. Ryan smiled, then turned on his heel and walked back to his truck.

Anna closed the front door and let the peace of the empty, yet familiar, house fill her soul. It was blessedly warm, and she briefly wondered who had paid the utilities to keep the furnace and electricity running since Aunt Theresa's passing. Regardless, she was safe here. After wandering through the main floor of the house—filled with worn-out furniture and walls that desperately needed a fresh coat of paint—Anna headed up the staircase, allowing memories of her childhood to flood her heart and mind. She found herself upstairs standing in her aunt's bedroom, tears gathering in her eyes as the grief of her passing hit her again. Someone had obviously kept the house clean and boxed up all the clothing and personal items from the bathroom. But the quilt on the queen-sized bed was the same one Anna remembered snuggling under as a child. Closing the door of the room filled with memories, Anna took a deep breath before turning to another bedroom: the one that had been hers as a child. She knew that Aunt Theresa had planned to turn it into a guest bedroom when Anna left for college, but she was surprised to see some familiar touches. The photo prints of plumeria blossoms that were Anna's favorite flower were still on the wall, in the same place that she had hung them during her last year of high school. Her desk and chair were still in the corner, but the bed and duvet were new, as was the rug on the floor. The room was small, but held great comfort for Anna. Needing to feel her aunt's presence, she went back to the master bedroom and gathered the old quilt off the bed. And when she had brushed her teeth and pulled on some warm pajamas, Anna wrapped herself up in the quilt, inhaled deeply to catch the faint scent of her aunt's perfume, and allowed the nostalgia and love she still felt in the house hold her close as she drifted to sleep.

* * *

The next morning, after making her way with bleary eyes to the outdated kitchen, Anna was relieved to find some instant coffee in the cupboard. It certainly wasn't the best cup of coffee she'd ever had, but the caffeine worked its way into her system, helping her wake up. As she contemplated how to spend her morning, there was a knock at the door, followed by the bark of a dog. Curious but cautious, Anna made her way to the front door and looked through the peephole. There on her front porch stood an older woman, dressed in a warm coat. In her arms she held what appeared to be a box full of food, and at her feet sat a large dog that looked like a cross between a German Shepherd and something else. The woman and the dog both had friendly looking faces, so Anna swallowed her nerves and opened the door to greet her visitors.

"Oh hello, Anna dear! I do hope we didn't wake you, but Samson was desperate to come home," said the strange woman, with a welcoming voice.

The dog bounded past Anna and ran through the house before

going to lie down on a dog bed beside the couch that she had not noticed the night before.

"Ah, there we go, he's so happy to be back." There was an air of satisfaction in the woman's voice—the woman who still had not introduced herself. But Anna surmised the dog must be Samson.

"I'm sorry, Ma'am, but who are you? And whose dog is that?" Anna asked, stepping back to allow the older woman to come in out of the cold.

The woman chuckled. "Oh goodness, I'm sorry, I'm Sally Tisdale, your next-door neighbor. I moved in two years ago and your Aunt Theresa and I became very dear friends. When she fell sick, she asked me to keep an eye on the house and care for Samson until you came home." A sad look crossed Sally's face, as she set the box of food on the ground and took off her jacket. "Theresa knew you would come back eventually. I don't know much but I know she was worried about you, that's why she told her lawyer it was so important that he find you and make sure you knew you always had a home here. She wanted you to be safe and happy."

Anna was floored by what Sally said. And the guilt that flooded her heart, knowing she was not there when her aunt needed her the most, threatened to crush her. Every time Anna talked about going to visit Aunt Theresa, Tim found a way to keep her in California. It was scary to realize how he had used fear and manipulation to make Anna follow his demands. The destruction to her self-esteem, and the loss of all her relationships, had broken her spirit for a long time.

Oblivious to the turmoil in Anna's heart, Sally continued, "Anna, my dear, she adored you. She was so confident you would do well at college and become a teacher like you always planned. Her dream was always for you to come back to Portland and re-start your life here. She adopted that silly dog, Samson, just last year, right before she got sick. He's a love of a dog, but I'm afraid I just can't keep him."

Sally patted Anna's shoulder, then picked up the box of food from the floor and walked into the kitchen. Anna followed her in a daze, trying to process everything Sally had said, as well as her own guilt and pain over the distress she was certain her aunt must have felt.

In the kitchen, Sally started to unpack the box, which was full of the basics: milk, bread, coffee, some apples, and various vegetables. Over her shoulder she told Anna, "There should still be some meat in the freezer, assuming you aren't a vegetarian. I put in a couple of casseroles earlier this week, so there should be enough to get you through a couple of days. Oh, and I checked the food in the pantry and it's all fresh." Sally paused in her work, looking at Anna fondly. "It's hard to believe she's been gone three weeks already. The cancer took her so quickly, I suppose it was a blessing she didn't suffer for long. One day she was here, working in the yard and playing crib with me, the next she was in a hospital bed, making me promise to watch Samson and keep the house maintained until you came home. I have to say, I was quite happy to see that porch light on this morning. Theresa's lawyer told me you had a key, but I had no idea when you would actually arrive. It's good to see life in the house again."

Unable to form a response, Anna simply walked over to the woman who obviously loved her aunt almost as dearly as she had and pulled her into a hug. She hoped that Sally would be able to share stories about her aunt over the last few years and was incredibly thankful that Aunt Theresa had such a good friend.

"Sally, I don't even know what to say. Thank you for the food, and for caring for the house and Samson."

"Oh, nonsense, my dear, it's my pleasure. I'll leave you to settle in and get acquainted with Samson. He's a friendly mutt and loves to run in the backyard." Sally walked toward the front door. She opened it and paused, looking back thoughtfully at Anna who had followed her. "Your aunt thought you might be in some kind of trouble down in California. Now, I won't pry but if you ever need someone to talk to, I'm here. You're not alone, Anna." With a loving smile and a wave, Sally closed the door, leaving Anna by herself once more.

She wandered back into the kitchen, made a fresh cup of coffee, and looked at the big dog who had moved to sit in the kitchen by the back door, and was looking at her curiously. "Well, Samson, I guess it's you and me boy. I've never had a dog, so be nice okay?" She opened the door, and with a happy bark Samson ran down into the backyard, and raced around the open space, kicking up snow everywhere. A spontaneous laugh came from Anna, as the pure joy in the dog's behavior lifted her spirits. Nothing had gone as she had expected it to since she arrived in Portland. Fear that Tim may find her still lingered in her mind, and she knew she might someday have to address the horrific events that had forced her to run. At least for now, Anna was content to stand in the peaceful space of the kitchen, watching Samson play and feeling her aunt's spirit fill her with a strength she hadn't felt in a very long time.

4

Chapter 3

Ryan let out a massive yawn as he stumbled into his small kitchen that morning. He had not slept for more than half an hour at a time, tossing and turning, his head filled with thoughts of Anna. She had seemed so vulnerable last night and yet so easily trusting of him, for which he was very thankful. He was still surprised at his visceral reaction to her; never had a woman stirred such a strong protective instinct within him.

As he drank a cup of coffee, feeling the hot jolt of caffeine start to wake up his mind, his thoughts drifted to his mom. Molly Carlisle had been harping on at Ryan and his brother to "grow up and settle down" for a while now, no matter how many times Ryan reminded her that he was only thirty-two. He knew she had worried for a long time whether Ryan would ever find his way after his injury in college, but now working with Jake and running the bar was the most fulfilling thing Ryan had ever done—next to soccer. As for the settling down part, for the first time ever Ryan now found himself wondering if he could be capable of a real relationship. For so many years he had satisfied his physical needs with meaningless one-night stands. Anything to avoid turning out like his dad; a cheater and a loser who left a woman with two kids and nothing else. He was desperate to avoid causing, or receiving, the deep pain that his mother had carried for so many years, pain that came from love.

Ryan knew he had the same Irish charm and good looks as his father, and he couldn't help but wonder if that charm meant he was also destined to hurt any woman he fell for. So, he consciously avoided falling in the first place. The irony was, his older brother, Noah, was just as good looking and charming, but was a die-hard romantic who believed in true love and desperately wanted to find his soul mate. The two brothers were close, despite their differences, and never missed a chance to tease each other mercilessly about their dating experiences. Now, after so many years spent believing he would never end up in a relationship, Ryan found himself questioning that belief. Wanting it to be wrong, wanting to be involved with a specific someone.

After he finished his coffee and had a quick shower, Ryan shot off a text to Jake to let him know about Anna coming in to start training later today. Briefly, he wondered if he should have talked to Jake before offering the job to Anna, but then he realized he didn't really care what his friend thought. He was going to do whatever it took to take care of Anna, and that meant helping her get a job. The fact that he would then be able to see her all the time and hopefully explore his feelings was just a bonus.

RYAN: Hey, just a heads-up, last night after you left, I hired a girl to help at the pub. She's coming in with me this afternoon to get some training.

Ryan watched the '...' that meant Jake was replying, but when no text came through he wasn't surprised to see Jake's name light up when his phone rang.

"Hey, what's up?" Ryan answered the call, trying to sound nonchalant.

"What's up? Ryan, what the fuck! You hired someone last night without even talking to me first? Who is she, some bar bimbo you took home last night? I thought you were closing early. And why the hell did you hire some stranger without checking with me first, dude. We're partners remember?" Instantly, Ryan felt defensive of his actions, but more importantly of Anna.

"Back off, asshole. She's not a bimbo, okay? Look. This girl came in last night looking for coffee. We got to talking, she just moved back and needs a job, and we need help. Simple as that. You can check her out this afternoon, but don't be a dick."

Silence filled the line, long enough that Ryan started to squirm, wondering just how pissed his friend really was. When Jake finally answered, his voice was calmer, but Ryan could still hear the thread of frustration.

"Look, Ry, I'm not going to be a dick. But this is OUR bar, which means we make the decisions together. Not to mention, in all our years of friendship, I've never known you to care enough about a woman to want to help her, much less defend her like that. So, tell me why you're acting like this. What is so special about her?"

Ryan sighed as he tried to figure out how to explain the feeling in his gut without sounding like a romantic loser. "I don't know, there's just something about her. I just need to help her, you know? I couldn't stop this feeling of wanting to take care of her even if I tried. It's messing with me."

Jake barked out a laugh. "Ah, I get it now. A woman finally

got to you, man. Oh, how the mighty have fallen!"

Ryan didn't even try to deny Jake's statement. How could he when his best friend was right, Anna had found a way past his defenses. "Yeah, whatever, I'm giving her a ride to the bar this afternoon. Look, Jake, I think something bad happened to her in the past, so be cool."

Jake's tone sobered. "Bad like what? Are we in for some trouble?"

"Nah, I don't think so. Just, she has these bruises on her wrist and she seemed super nervous at first. I don't know what happened, but I'm going to find out, and I'm going to take care of her if she'll let me."

"Okay, I get it—I'll be cool. And, Ry? I'm happy to hear that you might have finally found someone who gets to you."

Ryan smiled. "Yeah, yeah, thanks. Cut the mushy shit. I'll see you later okay?"

Hanging up, Ryan felt a burst of energy at the thought of seeing Anna in a few hours. Needing to release it somehow, he impulsively grabbed his keys and gym bag before sliding his feet into some running shoes. Hopefully, an hour or so of pushing his body to its physical limits at the gym would help Ryan regain some control before he saw Anna again.

* * *

Freshly showered, with muscles that still quivered from exhaustion, Ryan pulled up to Anna's house. He sat in his truck for a minute and tried to gather his thoughts. He still couldn't quite wrap his head around how strong his attraction to Anna was. More so, he was shocked by how desperately he wanted to get closer to her, learn everything about her, and most importantly keep her safe from whatever demons she faced. This protective instinct was a new emotion for Ryan, and he still struggled to make sense of it.

When Anna got to the truck and knocked softly on the window, he looked up in surprise before grinning widely. He was pleased to see Anna's expression soften into a smile in return, as he reached over to open the door.

"Hey! Climb in, the truck is a lot warmer than it is outside." Ryan hoped his tone was casual enough, the last thing he wanted to do was spook Anna into doubting the comfort she was beginning to exhibit around him.

"Thank you, Ryan, I really appreciate the ride. I swear I'm going to look for a car as soon as I can, and I did figure out the bus route as well, so you don't have to drive me every day. I don't want to be a bother," Anna replied. She looked down at her hands as she spoke, her voice hesitant, almost as if she expected Ryan to be frustrated with her. He reached over with his hand, covering her own small ones and gave them a gentle squeeze. He tried to infuse his voice with calm reassurance before answering.

"Look, sweetheart, I wouldn't have offered a ride if I didn't want to. I promise, you're not bothering me, I'm happy to help."

Ryan hoped the endearment which had just slipped out didn't push Anna too far, but he needed her to know that giving her a ride and spending time with her, was exactly what he wanted to be doing.

"Whenever you're ready to buy a car, I'll come with you. Car salesmen can be so damn sneaky, especially with single women. I want you to get something safe and reliable, but not pay a stupid amount for it, okay?"

Anna was silent, so silent that Ryan worried he had crossed a line by trying to insert himself into her life so quickly. When he glanced over at her, that worry turned into full blown concern when he saw tears slowly rolling down her face. Quickly, Ryan unbuckled his seat belt and slid over on the bench seat so he was close enough to hesitantly touch Anna's face. He brushed away a tear, grateful when she didn't shy away from him.

"I'm so sorry, Anna. I didn't mean to scare you."

Anna pressed her cheek into Ryan's hand, reaching up to cover it with her own. Her voice quavered, but had a thread of courage when she said, "You didn't. I promise I'm not sad or scared. It's just, well, it's been a long time since anyone cared about me as much as you do. And we just met, so it feels a little crazy. I'm sorry for crying like that, I'm just so thankful for everything."

Ryan let out a breath he had not even realized he was holding. "Oh, thank god. I was worried... I thought... I mean... I know I can be pushy, but I really do just want to be there for you. Please, let me be there for you." He stuttered over his words, which was so unlike his usual confident self, he felt totally mixed up inside.

"I'll try, thank you," she replied, immediately reassuring him.

Their drive to work after that was much calmer, as Anna asked some questions about her work duties at the bar, and Ryan told her about some of the craft beers they had on tap and the different breweries they worked with. All too soon they were at the parking lot of The Lucky Strike. Jake's car was already there, so Ryan knew his time alone with Anna had come to an end for now. He only hoped Jake would remember his promise and give her whatever space and time she needed to feel safe and comfortable. And Ryan vowed he would soon find out what had happened to make her so distrustful and nervous in the first place.

* * *

A couple of hours later, Anna found herself wrapping a waitress apron around her waist and trying to settle her nerves. So far, the afternoon had gone well, with Ryan taking care of her employment paperwork and showing her the basics of the bar. She knew that once Ryan started teaching her how to work behind the bar, instead of just waitressing, the work would be a lot more complicated. She had met Jake, whom she learned was not only Ryan's partner in owning the bar, but also his best friend. She was shocked at how quickly she found herself relaxing with Jake, but maybe it made sense given how close he and Ryan were. Objectively, she could see that Jake was an extremely handsome man, with dark wavy hair and warm eyes. But even his muscular body didn't stir up feelings in her core like Ryan's carefree Irish looks. His ginger hair and dancing blue eyes, that seemed to connect with everyone he spoke to, warmed Anna in a way she had not felt in a very long time. Every now and then she found herself gazing at him, and marveling at how lucky she had been to stumble into his pub when she arrived in Portland. Someday Anna hoped she would find a way to repay him for all his kindness.

Now, faced with the prospect of having to interact with strangers and put herself out there, Anna was wracked with fear and doubt. Tim had methodically cut her off from all her friends and had manipulated her with fear and false promises into only leaving the house to go to gatherings with his group of associates. Those men had scared Anna with their lecherous behavior, made worse by the awful, revealing outfits Tim had forced her to wear. Tonight would be the first time in a long time that Anna was in a social venue, without Tim hovering beside her.

At first everything went smoothly. Anna was able to remain calm and, she hoped, friendly enough with the customers. Her nerves bubbled to the surface if she needed to approach groups of men rather than groups of women, but she forced herself to keep her head up and work through it. Ryan's warm smile every time she went to the bar to collect a drink order certainly helped. And even when she was not up at the bar, she could feel his eyes on her. Feeling how aware he was of her, how considerate he was, helped Anna relax as the evening went on.

Waiting at the bar for Ryan to finish with a customer and pour the drinks she was waiting for, Anna was caught off guard when a cold hand grabbed her waist and a man, whose breath reeked of alcohol, leaned in close. "Hey, hot stuff, how about you serve my needs next." Anna was paralyzed by fear and couldn't respond—couldn't move away. Then, as quickly as the man had been there, he was gone, and Ryan was beside her, cautiously touching her shoulders to turn her toward him. She met his eyes and slowly the roaring in her ears died down enough that she could hear him.

"...God, Anna, I'm so sorry. Are you okay? As soon as I saw him head toward you, I came over. I'm so fucking sorry I wasn't there fast enough. You're safe here, you know that, right? You're safe with me."

The concern on his face was matched by the fury in his voice, but Anna knew that his anger was not directed at her. She let him pull her into his strong embrace, chanting in her own head *safe, safe, safe, safe, safe.*

Ryan led Anna into the small office at the back of the pub. He sat her down on the small couch, careful to give her space and not sit too close to her. "Anna, I know you've gone through something in your past, and I'm not asking you to tell me about it now, but I am telling you, you can trust me. You can trust Jake, his fiancé Callie, and our friends. We're the good guys, and if you let us, we'll be here for you."

The release of adrenaline, combined with Ryan's gentle but unwavering support, did more to help Anna relax than anything else. She slowly slid toward him on the couch and with a soft sigh, laid her head on his shoulder. Carefully, he wrapped his arm around her waist, and she let herself be tucked in close to his side, reveling in the warmth of the steady beat of his heart. They stayed that way quietly for a few minutes before Anna sat up. The trust and comfort she felt with Ryan was unlike anything she had ever felt, and she wanted to believe in those feelings, but she had seen too much and been hurt too badly to open up to him completely.

With a deep breath, she decided to share just a small piece of her story. "I know you're a good guy. It's crazy, we only just met, but I do know I can trust you. I can't tell you everything just yet, but you deserve to know the truth, I saw some bad stuff happen back in California. I guess it spooked me a lot."

Ryan looked deeply into her eyes for a minute, so deep she felt he could see the truth etched on her soul. But instead of pressing her further, he simply nodded and pulled her back in for a hug.

"Thanks for telling me, Anna. I've got to get back out there, but take as long as you need before you come back out, okay?"

Anna nodded, relieved to hear she didn't have to go back to work right away. When the door closed softly behind him, she sagged back into the couch. The weight that had been lifted when she had opened up to Ryan was only a fraction of the burden she carried, yet she felt lighter than she had in years.

* * *

Out in the main bar area Ryan was relieved to see Jake had things under control. He realized the bar had been the last thing on his mind when he had taken Anna to the office. He had been singularly focused on her comfort and safety, and his need to comfort her. The intensity of that emotion made him pause for a moment, as he let it sink in. Okay, he had been starting to feel a desire to settle down and maybe try his hand at a real relationship, but never in a million years had Ryan anticipated ever falling so deeply and so quickly for any woman. Especially one he had yet to even kiss. As Ryan stood by the bar, deep in thought, he didn't notice Callie walk up to him until she touched his arm, a concerned look in her eyes.

"Ryan, is everything alright? You look lost or something."

Ryan startled then quickly recovered with an easy grin and pulled Callie in for a hug. He loved her like the sister he never had, and he was so happy she and Jake had found their way to each other. Callie was a badass doctor who had chosen love over her messed up family, who valued appearances more than their daughter's happiness. She had stayed true to who she was and built a career and a life doing what she loved, with the man she loved.

"Hey, Cal. I'm fine. Are you here for the night? I just replaced the peach ale keg if you want a drink."

Callie's eyes were examining him closely, and Ryan had to fight not to take a step back from the intensity of her speculation. "We'll get to the beer later. First, why don't you man up and tell me what's got you so deep in thought with that troubled look on your handsome face. Is everything alright with the bar?"

With a flash of inspiration Ryan realized that Callie might be just what Anna needed. Maybe it would be easier for her to relax and open up to a female friend.

"Yeah it's fine. Nothing to worry about. I just, well, I met this girl, and I think she might be in trouble, but she's scared and doesn't want to tell me why. I don't want to push her, but damn I can't help wanting to protect her. It's fucked up." He scrubbed his hands through his hair, making it even messier than before.

Callie laughed gently before pulling Ryan in for a hug. "You big softy. I knew it would happen someday; you've fallen for someone! She must be amazing."

Ryan chuckled. "Yeah, I think she is. But she's spooked, especially around guys. Some drunk grabbed her tonight and she freaked out. She's in the back office calming down now."

Callie frowned. "That poor girl. I have seen far too many women come into the ER, scared to see a male doctor so they wait for hours to see me or Mel. Most of them have some big scary dude pick them up, and it breaks my heart to see them leave, knowing they might be in danger at home. But I can't help them if they don't want help, and it might be the same with your girl. When she feels safer around you, maybe she'll tell you what happened. Look, why don't I go back and talk to her? Let her know you're not the only good person in Portland." Callie gave him a gentle nudge. "You get back to work before Jake goes nuts."

Ryan breathed deeply and smiled his agreement. He hoped that Callie would be the perfect person to help Anna believe she was safe around Ryan and Jake and their friends. Maybe a female friend was exactly what she needed right now. With a grateful nod to Callie, he headed back behind the bar, but his watchful gaze kept going back to the hall that led to the office, hoping to see Anna walk through it soon.

* * *

Anna had managed to calm her nerves and pull together the conflicting emotions of fear and desire that Ryan's closeness had sparked. She was shocked, and more than a little confused at how she felt around him; it felt strange to trust a man so easily and even more so to be attracted to him. Her relationship with Tim had turned her into a shell of her former self, scared of everything and everyone—except for Ryan it seemed.

A knock on the office door was followed quickly by it opening, and a beautiful woman with blonde hair pulled up in a ponytail, poked her head through. "Hey, Anna. I'm Callie, Jake's fiancée. Can I come in? Ryan mentioned you were back here and could maybe use a friend."

Anna stood dumbfounded, looking at Callie with what she was certain was a stupid look on her face. This woman wanted to get to know her, be her friend, just because of something Ryan had said? How was this happening, how did she go from scared and alone, to surrounded by people who wanted to help her, in just a couple of days? Recovering from her surprise, she quickly smiled and gestured at Callie to come in.

"Umm, hi, nice to meet you. Of course you can come in." Anna blushed, uncertain if Ryan had shared why she had needed to hide in the office. "I just got spooked by some creep, but I'm okay now, really."

Callie sat down on the couch beside her. "Oh man, some guys are so gross. I'm sorry that happened. I promise Jake and Ryan are so careful to watch for any jerks that somehow get in here. Alcohol makes some men think they can get away with anything." She paused and looked at Anna thoughtfully. "Look, Ryan didn't say much, but he obviously cares about you. That makes you important to me and to Jake as well. So, if there is anything you need, please just ask. You're not alone, not now that Ryan Carlisle has decided to make you part of our crazy group of friends."

With a warm smile, Callie pulled Anna in for a brief hug before releasing her and reaching over to grab a piece of paper and a pen from the desk. "Here's my number. I work weird hours in the ER, but just text me and I'll get back to you as soon as I can."

Anna looked from the paper to Callie, dumbstruck by this act of kindness from a woman she had just met.

"Thank you, really, this is so kind. It's been a tough couple of years, but I finally feel like things are going to be okay." She could feel tears beginning to pool in her eyes and quickly tried to blink them away.

Callie touched her leg gently. "Anna, I think I might know what you've been through. I won't pry, but I will tell you that you are completely safe with Ryan, and with me and Jake. If you ever want to talk, I'm here, or I can easily connect you with some of the domestic violence counselors we have at the hospital where I work."

Anna's eyes widened in shock at how perceptive Callie had been, which was quickly followed by a stab of fear. Did Ryan also know she had been in an abusive relationship? She mumbled softly in response, overcome. "Thank you, Callie. I don't know what else to say. Just, can you not tell anyone, I wouldn't want people to think I'm weak or a helpless victim or something."

Callie's voice was gentle and went a long way to soothe the shame Anna had lived with for so long. "Say no more. My lips are sealed. But if my assumption is right, you are a victim. And that doesn't make you weak. In fact, it makes you incredibly strong because you survived, and you got out. Be proud of that okay? And remember, you don't have to be alone anymore."

Anna felt strength flow through her at Callie's words. It was crazy how powerful a statement from a virtual stranger could be, but somehow Anna found herself believing every word. She was not alone anymore.

5

Chapter 4

Over the next week, Anna found herself settling into a comfortable routine. Her mornings were spent walking and playing with Samson, and slowly sorting through Aunt Theresa's house. There was a lot that she planned to donate to the local thrift shop, and more things that were too far gone to be donated and would have to be taken to the dump. Her afternoons were spent at The Lucky Strike, where she was feeling more comfortable waiting on customers, but was happiest behind the bar with Ryan. There was something about having the long wooden bar top between her and everyone else that gave her a sense of security that felt foolish but couldn't be denied.

Her friendship with Callie was also steadily growing, as Callie spent most of her free time hanging out at the bar. After so many years without female friendship, Anna cherished this time. Anna loved the story of how Callie and Jake fell in love; it amazed her how Jake and Ryan could be such strong, sexy, alpha males but also have a softer side and treated women with such respect.

As her comfort around Ryan, Jake, and Callie grew, so did

her feelings of attraction to Ryan. It had been so long since a man had shown care and affection towards her, and she began to long to feel the touch of a sensual caress from a partner, or better yet a lover.

Every Tuesday, the guys closed the bar for the day. They both needed a day off to rest, relax, and do something other than sling beers and chat up customers. This week, Jake and Ryan had headed off to the gym in the morning, and Callie had come over to help Anna get the house cleaned up.

As the two women carried boxes full of items to sort through down the stairs and into the living room, the conversation turned to Ryan.

"I've never seen him look at someone the way he looks at you. I know you say you aren't interested in a relationship, but you have to agree that Ryan is amazing and it's pretty obvious you're attracted to each other."

Anna put her hands up, in a feeble attempt to deflect the conversation away from her growing attraction to Ryan. "I know he's a great guy, I'm just not ready. No matter how amazing Ryan is. If my ex ever found me..." She trailed off. By now, she had accepted that Callie knew she had been in a toxic relationship.

"Anna, I don't want to pry, but haven't you realized by now that all we want to do is be there for you? Maybe the guys and I can help keep you away from your ex, but you have to let us."

Anna sighed. She knew Callie was coming from a place of caring, but she couldn't bring herself to confess the truth about Tim. She was so scared that if her new friends found out how stupid she had been, falling into an abusive relationship with such a powerfully evil man, they would look at her differently, judge her, not want her around anymore.

"I can't tell you how happy I am to have you as a friend. I know you want to help, but there are things I just can't talk about yet." Anna grabbed the nearest box of things she had carted downstairs, and started rifling through it, desperate to change the subject. "So, are we ready to start digging through this stuff?"

Callie looked at Anna for a moment before seeming to accept that the conversation was over for now.

"You're right, there's a lot to do. I think we need some help." Callie raised her eyebrows. "Why don't you text Ryan? With the bar closed today, I'm sure he and Jake could help after their workout. Let's get some eye candy over here, the boys can flex their muscles and we can sit back and watch."

Laughing, Anna rolled her eyes at Callie's idea. But inside she shivered as the vision of Ryan shirtless and sweaty danced in her head.

"Okay, I'll text him."

* * *

Over at the gym, Jake and Ryan were in the boxing ring sparring, to release some pent-up energy. Ryan was so distracted by thoughts of Anna that Jake was able to land a sucker punch that knocked him flat on his back. Groaning on the floor, he opened his eyes to see his best friend standing over top of him, with his hand stretched out ready to help him get up on his feet. Walking over to get some water, Jake followed and looked at Ryan closely.

"What is it about this woman that has you so tied up, man? In all the years I've known you, I've never seen you get close enough to someone to care like this."

The words stung, mostly because he was right. As best friends, Jake was all too familiar with Ryan's playboy past, and knew the reason behind it thanks to a drunken confession one night in college. He didn't agree with Ryan's opinion and had tried to tell him many times that he was nothing like his dad, but Ryan had always refused to take the chance that he was. So how could he possibly explain that he had no idea what was different about Anna, or why he was so focused on her. He knew it made no sense, but somehow over the last couple of weeks her happiness had become his priority. He couldn't stop thinking of her and was taking more cold showers trying to calm his desires than he had since he was a horny teenager.

"I don't know, I can't explain it. Look, I didn't give you a hard time when you fell for Callie faster than a ton of bricks, so just back off okay? I like Anna. It doesn't make sense to me, but I do." Ryan could hear the protective tone in his voice but didn't care. Anna brought that out in him.

Jake raised his hands in defense. "Okay, dude, I'm not trying to be an ass. It's just weird watching you fawn all over her. But if she is the one who can tame the beast, then that's cool with me. Callie loves her, she's a hard worker at the bar, and you're happy. It's all good."

Ryan nodded and didn't say anything else. Taming the beast, yeah that was pretty much what was happening. So, when he got Anna's text, asking if he and Jake could help her and Callie to move some furniture and boxes in the house that afternoon, there was no hesitation. If helping Anna led to sweaty, shirtless work, well, maybe that would be enough of an enticement for Anna to let him move their friendship a little closer to something more.

* * *

Several hours later, dusty, and tired, Anna and Callie dropped to the couch in Anna's living room. Reaching down to scratch Samson on the head, Anna let out a deep breath of contentment.

"I have to say, Callie, you were right. Having the guys come over to help really did make the day a lot more productive. I can't believe how much we got done."

"And the view didn't hurt now did it?" Callie nudged Anna playfully.

No, it certainly had not been a hardship to watch the guys work today, their muscles bulging as they carried heavy boxes and pieces of furniture around. As the men in question walked into the room, Anna's heart sped up watching Ryan pull the bottom of his shirt up to wipe his face, exposing strong abs and that delicious V of muscle low on his torso, all dusted with blond hair. When she realized that Ryan had caught her stare and was grinning impishly at her, Anna knew she blushed a bright red, deepening her embarrassment at being caught gawking. But how could she not stare when he was so damn sexy!

"Okay, I think that's the last of the junk from the attic. It's all loaded in my truck, so Cal and I can drop it off at the dump tomorrow." Jake sank down on the couch next to his fiancée and pressed a kiss to the side of her head.

Callie giggled and leaned away. "Ewww, babe, you stink!"

"What? My sweaty man aroma doesn't turn you on?" Jake pulled her into a tight hug, as they both laughed.

The playfulness between Jake and Callie was so filled with love, Anna was starting to feel uncomfortable, like a third wheel, until she noticed Ryan smiling affectionately at his friends. His connection to the happy couple was also tangible, but, when Anna looked closely, she could see what felt suspiciously like longing in his eyes. Could it be he was looking for the same kind of love Jake and Callie were blessed to have? Anna found herself wistfully wondering what it would be like to be so loved and cherished by someone like Ryan. How incredible that would be.

Jumping up with nervous energy, Anna felt compelled to push away her feelings, as she worried the others could sense her growing attraction to Ryan. The last thing she needed right now was any awkwardness between them. After all, her job and her only real friendships were on the line.

"Well, the place looks amazing. I can't believe how much we got cleaned up and fixed. I really appreciate your help."

Callie stood up from the couch and stretched her arms up high. "I'm glad we got so much done for you, but I think Jake and I need to head out. We don't get many days off together, and our own to-do list is massive."

Jake stood up, wrapping his strong arms around Callie's waist. He leaned down with a mock growl, nuzzling into her neck as he muttered, "I know what is on my list to do today, gorgeous..."

"Get a goddamn room, guys, or at least wait until you're out of the house before you jump each other." Ryan slapped Jake on the back in a typical guy embrace and pulled Callie in for a gentler hug. "I'll see you later, I'm just going to grab a quick drink."

Anna glanced at him as he headed toward her kitchen, seeming so at ease in her home. Something about him being there felt incredibly comfortable to her. Turning back to the front door, where Callie and Jake stood ready to leave, Anna twisted her hands together, suddenly overcome with gratitude.

"Thank you so much for helping me. I'm sorry I took up so

much of your day."

Callie pulled her in for a hug. "Don't be silly, we're friends. Helping each other is what we do, and we were happy to be here." Her gentle chastising eased some of the worry Anna was feeling, but she still felt unworthy of their time and kindness.

Closing the door after they had left, Anna took in a deep breath as her entire body tingled with the awareness that Ryan was standing close behind her.

"So, what's next?"

She turned to see him leaning against the wall, arms folded in front of him. He had a relaxed look about him and seemed to have absolutely no intention of leaving.

"I was going to get started on painting some walls, but you don't have to stay. You've already done so much and I'm sure you had better plans for your day off."

"Sweetheart, what kind of man would I be if I left you to paint this place by yourself?" Nudging her playfully, he continued to tease her, "Besides, I need your arms to still be functioning tomorrow night."

Anna's breath sped up as dirty thoughts of why Ryan would want her arms tomorrow night filled her head. She could tell his mind went down that sensual path as well when his eyes grew dark and he looked at her with what couldn't be mistaken as anything but lust in his eyes.

Anna broke the tension with a nervous laugh. "Right. My arms. For carrying all those trays of drinks."

Ryan pushed up from his stance on the wall, and Anna was struck by how close he was. So close he could just dip his head down and kiss her. Would he? She wasn't sure, just as she wasn't sure if she was ready for that. He seemed to sense her hesitation and backed away with an easy smile.

"Tell you what. You spring for pizza, and let me choose the tunes we listen to, and I'll stay and paint. Sound fair?"

Feeling slightly more even-keeled with that casual offer, Anna smiled. "Okay, I can go along with that. But I swear, if you tell me you want pineapple on your pizza or play rap music, I'll have to kick your cute butt out of here." It was a shock to her, how easy flirting with him was.

With an exaggerated swagger, Ryan walked past Anna toward the living room. Giving his butt a shake, he grinned over his shoulder. "I'll have you know this cute butt thinks fruit on pizza is an abomination, and the only rap music worth listening to came out two decades ago. How about pepperoni and mushrooms on the pizza? Keep it simple."

"Perfect."

6

Chapter 5

Over the next several hours, Ryan helped Anna to tape off and paint the kitchen, hallway, and living room. They only stopped for a quick dinner break, devouring the entire pizza. Anna felt more relaxed and happier than she had in years, laughing at Ryan's stories of all the crazy things he and his brother Noah had done as kids.

"Wow, your mom sounds like the most patient woman on earth." She playfully bumped Ryan with her shoulder as they sat side by side on the floor, leaning against one of the unpainted walls.

Ryan chuckled. "Yeah, she is amazing. Her strength is like nothing else. She raised us alone and worked tirelessly to not let us see how hard it was."

Anna sat pensively reflecting on her own childhood with Aunt Theresa. She too had never let it show how difficult it must have been, going from a single woman, to a woman who not only was grieving the loss of her sister, but was thrust into parenting a grieving child as well.

"My aunt was the same. I don't think I ever really thought

about how hard it was for her, trying to figure out how to parent a kid that wasn't even hers, but she never made me feel anything but loved. Makes me feel even more guilty for not being here for her."

Ryan reached over and took her hand. "She sounds like an amazing woman, who obviously loved you no matter what. Why did you lose touch? Why didn't you come home earlier?"

Anna's body instantly became tight with tension. Those were questions she was not ready to answer, and she could feel her defenses go up. She pulled her hand away and stood, moving toward the door in a not so subtle hint that the evening was over. Ryan followed silently, gathering his jacket and keys. When he was near enough, he cupped her chin and forced her to look up into his eyes.

"I'm sorry. I shouldn't have pried. I hope I didn't make you too uncomfortable."

Anna sighed. "No, Ryan, I'm the one who should be sorry. It's hard for me to talk about my past, but someday I hope I can. Just know that it's not you, it's me. You have made me so happy, and I feel so safe and cared for here with you and your friends. I just want to forget that my past ever happened for a little while longer."

Ryan pulled Anna against his chest, wrapping his arms tightly around her. "You can't ever escape your past. But it doesn't have to define you. I see you, Anna, and I really like what I see. Nothing is going to change that. And whenever you are ready to tell me your story, I'm ready to listen."

Anna felt tears gather behind her eyes, as she let herself fully relax into his warm embrace. His woodsy smell, a mixture of sweat and aftershave, was intoxicating, and the tightness of his arms around her felt strong and grounding. How could this man affect her so strongly, so quickly? She could feel herself falling for him with every minute they spent together.

After a few minutes, she gently pulled herself from his arms. He kept a hold of her hands as he looked down at her, with a smile and a look in his eyes that stirred a strong sense of longing inside her heart. "I really like spending time with you. Would you let me take you around town tomorrow before we go to work? Show you what has changed, we can grab some lunch; just relax and have fun."

"I'd love that." Anna blushed. "I really like spending time with you too."

With a quick smile, Ryan pressed a kiss to her forehead. When he pulled back, he brushed some hair behind her ear. "I don't want to freak you out, but I have to tell you this. I'm not normally so sappy, but I'm really glad you chose my bar to walk into the night you arrived. It's starting to feel like that was the beginning of something amazing." With a final gentle squeeze of her shoulders, he turned and left.

As she watched Ryan head down the snowy path to his truck, Anna marveled at how quickly her feelings for him were growing. The sexual attraction between them was undeniable, but more important than that was the comfort she felt around him. It had been so long since Anna was in a relationship, or even a friendship, that didn't come with controlling limits and expectations. Yes, Ryan was right. When she walked into The Lucky Strike that night, it was absolutely the start of something amazing.

Anna went about her evening chores in a daze. She let Samson out in the backyard, tidied up the kitchen and made sure all the doors and windows were locked. Her head was whirling with confusing thoughts. The chemistry between her and Ryan was at a point where it could no longer be denied. Tonight had shown her that, without a doubt, she could trust him to care for her, to put her needs first, and try to protect her. Fast on the heels of that hopeful thought, came the dose of reality—*But, what will he think of me if I tell him about Tim?*

Anna was terrified that by letting Ryan and his friends get close to her, she was putting them in danger. She had no idea how harsh Tim's retaliation over her leaving him could be, and the last thing she wanted was to expose her new friends to his dark and cruel life. Instinctively, she knew that Ryan would do everything he could to keep her safe. All she could do was hope that Tim would decide she was not worth the trouble and stay far away in California. Then, maybe, she could put her heart in Ryan's hands, and see if they could have a future filled with love.

* * *

The entire drive home, Ryan was so distracted by his thoughts he barely noticed the other cars on the road. Really, it was a miracle he made it without getting in an accident, he was so unaware of what was happening around him.

He was perplexed by the intense feelings and deep connection he felt for Anna. His entire life he had shied away from close relationships. Even Callie's friend Reagan, and Chase the singer and guitarist they hired to play at the bar regularly, were not what he would consider *close* friends. He didn't feel the same level of affection, protectiveness, and trust that he had with Jake and, by extension, Callie.

But what he felt for Anna was something different. The

emotions he experienced when he was around her, hell when he was just thinking about her, were so new for Ryan it should have freaked him out. Instead, he felt an overwhelming sense of peace. As if Anna was meant to be in his life, and he was meant to be in hers. He was starting to suspect that what he was experiencing was close to the feeling Jake had when he first met Callie. He decided that tomorrow, on their date to explore the city, he would push the limit slightly, to see if the growing attraction he knew was present between them could blossom into a real relationship.

The next day, Ryan pulled up to Anna's house, eager for their date to begin. As he walked up to her front door, he was floored by the sight of Anna standing on her porch waiting for him. Her cheeks were flushed from the cold, and her beautiful eyes sparkled with flecks of gold. But what was most noticeable and stirred something deep within Ryan was the new, confident, and happy smile on her face. Suddenly, beautiful Anna was absolutely stunning, and the sense of satisfaction he felt knowing he had played a part in bringing that smile onto her face was unlike anything else. Her excitement was infectious, and he found himself grinning back at her as she locked the door and reached for his hand in a way that felt so natural, he instantly wove his fingers in with hers.

"I'm really looking forward to this. Can we start with breakfast? I've wanted to try a maple bacon doughnut from that super popular place downtown ever since I saw a special about it on Food Network! Oh, and then let's walk down to the waterfront. I used to love wandering down by the river."

Ryan laughed at the child-like enthusiasm in her voice, it was so adorable he had to wrap his arm around her shoulders and tug her into his side, needing to feel her body against his.

"Your wish is my command, sweetheart, doughnuts and coffee is the breakfast of champions."

Anna eagerly climbed into the passenger side of his truck, but when she started to pull her seatbelt over her shoulder, Ryan stopped her with a hand on her leg. With a bashful look on his face, he asked, "Is it too forward of me to ask if you'll sit in the middle, next to me, so I can hold your hand?"

Anna reached out to touch his cheek where his Irish roots had made him blush. "What good is a bench seat if I'm all the way over here." She smiled coyly as she scooted over to the middle seat, and Ryan was thrilled that she seemed as affected as he was by the sizzling chemistry between them.

Ryan grinned and practically ran around to the driver's side, climbing in and reaching for Anna's hand as soon as he had his own seatbelt on. Thankfully, he had left the engine running when he got to her house, so the cab was toasty warm to combat the winter chill outside.

"Let's get that doughnut."

* * *

To Anna's delight, Ryan knew one of the owners at the iconic doughnut shop she had mentioned, who happened to be a regular at the pub. This let them bypass the crazy long lineup, that even on a cold morning snaked around the block. doughnuts and coffee in hand, they wandered down to the park that lined the Willamette river. As they passed under one of Portland's many bridges, they paused in the Japanese Historical Plaza to look around. Ryan stopped another couple to ask them to take a picture of them. Anna was thrilled she would have a photo to remember this near perfect morning. With the river in the background, Anna stood in his arms relishing the feel of his strong embrace. Even after the photo was taken, she stayed there, tucked in close to his side.

As they continued to explore the city, Anna felt herself relaxing more and more, so when Ryan asked how she ended up in California, this time she found it easy to answer, even if she still kept things vague.

"In high school I discovered I enjoyed tutoring, so I decided to become a teacher. Early education seemed like a great fit because I love kids. I applied to a lot of schools and, on a whim, I applied to California State University. The joke between Aunt Theresa and I was that if I went to CSU, she would learn how to surf when she came to visit. Aunt Theresa was so thrilled when I received my acceptance letter, but I almost didn't go. I was so sad about leaving her." Anna's voice trailed off as a wave of grief overcame her. "I left and I only came back to see her once. Then, I met Ti— my ex..." She stopped suddenly and pulled away, uncomfortable with how close she had come to revealing her past.

Ryan grabbed her arm and tugged her back to his side. She let him tip her chin up and lifted her gaze to meet his. His eyes were warm, but filled with concern. "Anna, I know something bad must have happened between you and your ex. You don't have to tell me what, not unless you want to. Just please know I'm not going anywhere, and I swear I will never hurt you."

Anna smiled softly, before settling back into his side. They walked in silence for a few moments before she spoke again. "So, what did you want to be when you grew up?"

Ryan was silent for a moment, and when she looked at him, Anna was surprised to see pain in his eyes.

"I'm sorry, I didn't mean to upset you."

"It's okay, sweetheart. I guess I have some stuff that's hard to talk about as well." He glanced down at her, before smiling gently. "Let's just say I had to give up my dreams. I'm happy now, but there's a part of me that will always miss what could have been."

Anna's heart ached to hear the pain in his voice. She pulled him in for a close embrace, knowing that he didn't need words of pity, just compassion and comfort.

"It sounds like we've both lost a piece of who we were." Anna's voice was quiet, thoughtful.

"Yeah," Ryan said with a nervous hitch. "Maybe we can find ourselves again, together."

Anna smiled, as she let the genuine emotion of his vulnerability wash over her.

"I'd like that."

7

Chapter 6

After lunch and a quick visit to the Portland Art Gallery, they returned to Anna's house, where they took Samson for a walk before she got changed for work. As they drove to the pub, Anna snuggled up against Ryan's side, enjoying the comfortable silence between them. The energy in the truck hummed with a sexual chemistry that was barely held back, yet she felt no pressure from him. He had been the perfect gentleman all day, letting her take the lead in how close they were. Anna struggled to remember why she had been so worried about starting a new relationship so soon after leaving Tim. Being in Ryan's arms, even in a casually affectionate embrace, felt so good it was all she could do to not let things progress. She longed to feel his lips on hers. Heated shivers went through her, straight to her core, when she let herself imagine what it would feel like to be intimate with Ryan. Would his respectful restraint disappear? Somehow, she knew he would be a considerate lover, but she also loved the thought of Ryan being a more dominant, erotically alpha partner in the bedroom.

They pulled into a parking space in the back of the pub, and reluctantly she slid out of the truck, immediately missing the closeness of Ryan's body. She followed him to the back door that led into the hallway behind the bar that held the bathrooms, office, and kitchen where he paused, one hand on the door, turned to her and said, "I had a really great time today, Anna. Thanks for letting me spend the day with you, and, I guess this sounds weird but thank you for trusting me. It means something to me that you're happy to be around me." Ryan ducked his head, running his hand through his hair nervously, as if he were worried about her reaction to his sweet words.

Anxious to show him that he had nothing to be concerned about, Anna reached up and placed her hands on his shoulders, a smile on her face. "Today was wonderful, I wish it didn't have to end."

She lifted on to her toes, to press a kiss to his soft, inviting lips. It was an impulsive move and one she didn't regret at all, until the sensual impact of Ryan's gaze after that simple kiss hit her. The sweet chemistry that had been slowly simmering between them all day seemed to grow exponentially, burning in his eyes, and threatening to overwhelm Anna. She stepped back and tried to regain control of her emotions and the situation before it went too far.

"I need to get to work. My new boss is a total slave driver." With what she hoped was a casual grin, Anna slipped past Ryan to go inside. She was both disappointed and relieved when he didn't try to stop her, but his parting shot had her grinning.

"Yeah, he sounds like a total asshole. You go to work, I'll set your boss straight... if, you'll take your dinner break with me?"

"Deal... Boss."

* * *

Ryan checked out front to make sure the new bartender was doing alright by himself, before heading into the back office to check in with Jake. So far, the new guy, Mark, had proven himself capable of handling the lunch time and afternoon crowds, but he still seemed to get overwhelmed by the frantic pace of the nighttime shift. Ryan hoped he would figure it out, he seemed like a solid dude, and had great references from the hotel bar he had worked at previously. The truth was, both Ryan and Jake could use the odd evening off. The Lucky Strike had been an instant success, for which they were grateful. But the non-stop pace of being open six days a week and drawing huge crowds—especially on the nights when Chase took the stage—was starting to get exhausting. Add in Jake's new engagement to Callie and the friends had found themselves in serious need of some solid help running the pub, so that they were not having to do everything themselves.

Sure enough, Ryan found his best friend with his head down, focused on the papers spread across the desk. He sat down on the couch that lined one wall of the small office and waited for Jake to come up for air.

When Jake finished, he leaned back with a satisfied sigh. "Hey, man, we're blowing past all of our targets for this month again. Shit, I love how successful we are, but, when I decided to open a pub, I never expected it would be so much goddamn work."

Ryan laughed at Jake's obviously sarcastic complaining. "Yeah, why the hell would it be hard work to open and run a kick-ass establishment. Serve drinks, smile, take their money. Easy."

"Shut up, you know what I mean. How's it going with the new staff out there?"

Jake's question felt more weighted than it should have, since Anna was one of those new staff. Ryan knew his friend was curious about what was happening between him and Anna, but he was not sure if he was ready to share, even with Jake.

"Mark's doing better behind the bar. He needs a few more night shifts with me before he will be ready to tackle it solo, and even then, I think I'll start him out with weeknights when it's a bit more chill. Chase's shows still need two of us tending bar, but I think you and I can partner with him on those nights so at least we get a bit of a break."

Jake stared at Ryan, refusing to let him get away without answering the question fully.

"And Anna?"

Ryan laced his fingers behind his head, trying to look casual. "Anna's doing great. She's not so skittish around strange guys anymore. She's a good waitress and is starting to learn how to pour some drinks."

"Yeah, I know her work is fine, stop playing dumb, Ryan. I want to know what's going on between YOU and Anna." Jake leaned forward as he spoke, a serious look coming over his face. "I'm not an idiot, when we were at her house the other day, I could tell there's something going on with you two. You're spending more time with her than I've ever seen you spend with any other woman before. No offense, but you are normally a *wham bam thank you ma'am* kinda guy. This time, as far as I can tell, there has not been any wham or bam yet. So, I'll ask you again. What the hell is going on between you and Anna?"

Standing up, Ryan started to pace the small office. Jake's words had touched a nerve, but he knew they were not meant in a bad way. It was true, Anna was the first woman he had been interested in and not immediately tried to get into bed with.

"Look, I don't know okay? She's different. I have no goddamn clue why, and trust me, that fact alone is messing with my head. But I really like her. She makes me feel things I've never felt before. Want things I have never wanted. But I know she has been through something awful, even if she won't tell me exactly what. So, I'm going slow. It's hard, but it will be worth it. I hope."

Jake nodded slowly, before letting a wide grin come over his face. "You've fallen for her. Damn. I never thought the day would come that Ryan Carlisle would be tamed. I'm happy for you."

"Yeah, yeah, fuck off." Ryan headed for the office door, knowing Jake had his back, like always.

"Get to work, Casanova," Jake called out as Ryan walked away.

Yes, just like always.

* * *

The first few hours of Anna's shift went smoothly. She spent most of her time serving customers, but when it wasn't too busy, she went behind the bar to learn how to mix drinks and practice pouring a pint of beer without having too much foam on top. The sexual innuendo of dealing with a *foamy head* was not lost on Anna, and the seductive wink that Ryan threw her way as he taught her how to avoid it, sent a wave of heat straight to her core.

It was a couple of hours before closing, and Anna was collecting a tray of drinks to take to a table of guys who had just come in. Clearly a sports team of some kind, they all had damp hair like they had just showered and were laughing and teasing each other loudly about who had scored the most points at their game. She put the glasses and pitcher of beer down in the middle of the table, and turned to go, proud of the fact that her nerves had not hit, even while some of the guys had lightly flirted with her. She felt secure knowing Ryan and Jake were watching out for her—she could feel Ryan's heated gaze on her all the time.

As Anna turned to go and check on her other tables, she glanced up at the front door when it opened. Even though she was on the other side of the pub, closer to the bar and nowhere near the door, her heart fell to her feet and she dimly heard her empty tray clattering to the ground as everything around her faded to a hazy nothingness. The man who had just walked in, tall and slender, with a neatly trimmed goatee had an arrogant look that was terrifyingly familiar as it swept the bar, thankfully not even pausing on Anna. While the tiny part of her brain that hadn't cowered in terror knew this man was not Tim, just an eerie lookalike, the rest of her had folded in utter panic. She couldn't avoid the flash of memories of Tim's icy expression and his cruel voice. Barely able to gulp in a breath, Anna turned and ran through the back hallway, past the kitchen and office, and straight out into the alley and the sharp, cold winter air. Gasping at the chill, she crouched down, wrapping her arms around her knees trying to warm herself and calm down. A few seconds later the back door banged open again, making her jump up in fear. But it was Ryan, a scared and worried look on his face. He ran over to Anna and without pausing pulled her tight against his chest. Only then did she feel the fear leave her with a deep shudder of relief.

"Anna? Sweetheart, what's wrong." The fear came through

loud and clear in Ryan's voice. "Talk to me, what are you doing out here shaking as if you've seen a ghost?"

Anna trembled, realizing the time had come to tell Ryan more of why she had left California in such a hurry. If she was going to trust this man, as a friend or as something more, he deserved to know what had happened, what could happen if Tim ever found her. Taking a deep breath, she began to speak, hating the fear-filled tremble she could hear in her voice.

"A guy came into the bar. He looked... I thought..." She trailed off, realizing she probably was not making any sense. Anna knew Ryan would never judge her for what she had been through, but still it was hard to finally reveal the shame and the fear that had choked her for so long. Like Callie had said, she was a victim—as much as she wished to pretend the last few years had not even happened and were just a bad dream.

"When I was in California, at CSU to get my teaching degree, I met someone: Tim. He seemed like a nice guy, charming even. We dated and things moved quickly. But then he changed. He started to get controlling. It came across as jealousy, concern, *'I'm just trying to help, baby',*" she said this last part in a scorn-filled imitation of a man's voice. "But soon he gave up all pretense of trying to be a good guy and just turned into an asshole. He was into some bad stuff, I didn't know exactly what at the time, but it involved drugs and some majorly scary dudes coming to the apartment late at night. He convinced me to drop out of school because he was jealous of how much time I spent in class, I lost my friends because he controlled my time and who I saw. I couldn't leave because he had convinced me to move in with him back in the beginning, so I had nowhere else to live. He made me believe that I needed him, and that no one else wanted me around anymore. I eventually stopped talking to Aunt Theresa except for once in a while because I was so embarrassed by what I had let my life become, and so damn terrified of what would happen if she figured out what my life was like and tried to get me to leave."

Anna pulled away from Ryan, instantly missing his warmth, but needing to move, feeling restless with the shame and grief that filled her.

"I knew what was going on, I knew I was in an abusive relationship. I've been to self-defense courses, I've read the articles, heard the stories. Hell, before I met Tim, I spent a month volunteering for a crisis support phone line, talking to other women who were in abusive relationships. And you know what? It is all bullshit. What they don't teach you is how fucking manipulative those bastards are. How they know exactly what to say and do, how far to push you before reeling you in, either with charm or with intimidation. You never learn how to notice the manipulation before it's too late, and you are in so deep you're drowning." Anna's voice caught on a sob. Ryan strode over to her and pulled her back into his arms. She sagged into his embrace, relieved that finally, someone knew her story. Someone had heard her.

Wrapped in his arms, warm and protected, Anna knew she had to continue. She had to tell Ryan everything that was in her heart, he deserved that and so much more.

"I'm scared, Ryan. I have these crazy feelings when I'm around you that make no sense, but I can't avoid them." Looking up into his eyes, she could see he wanted to respond, so she gently put her fingers over his lips. She had to get it out before she could stand to hear what he had to say. "Please know I never meant for this to happen. I didn't come to your bar looking for anything more than a cup of coffee that night. But meeting you turned my life around when it was at the darkest point. You helped me so much when I first got here. You gave me a job, you gave me friends, and you gave me someone I could trust. I know that might make me sound codependent or needy or something stupid like that, but it's the opposite for me. You are helping me feel strong again. At the same time, I am terrified of falling for someone, trusting someone again. It has nothing to do with you, and everything to do with how broken Tim made me."

Anna took a breath, steadying herself for Ryan's response. But she was unprepared for the tenderness in his gaze as he gently held her away so he could look into her eyes.

"Anna, you are the strongest woman I have ever met. You are no more broken than anyone else in this world. Don't you dare give that jackass any more power over your life. He's not here, you are, and I am. I see you, Anna Thorn, and I like what I see." Ryan's voice rang with sincerity, bringing soft tears to Anna's eyes. "I'm going to kiss you now. So that you can trust that I have those same crazy feelings that I don't want to avoid any more either."

Ryan tilted her head up, cupping her face with his large hands. Tentatively, Anna wrapped her arms around his strong shoulders, marveling at the power of his muscular body. This was a man who could make her feel so much, but a man who she instinctively knew would never use that power against her. As his mouth lowered to hers, she sucked in a gentle gasp of arousal. His lips brushed hers, gently at first, as if he were feeling for her readiness. When she pulled him closer that was all the signal he needed, and the kiss turned heated. Lips crushed together and tongues danced in perfect balance. Anna moaned into his mouth and Ryan's hands wound through her hair, tugging her head back gently so he could press kisses all over her mouth and down her neck. Returning to her lips, his kiss seemed to stop time. She no longer felt the cold around her, she was so lost in the heat of their embrace.

At the sound of a throat clearing behind them, Anna and Ryan jumped apart. It was Jake, smiling wryly at the two of them. "When Mark said you two had run outside like the devil was chasing you, I was worried for a minute. I guess the devil is just the one in your pants, Ryan."

Anna started to protest, feeling the need to defend Ryan's actions in abandoning his work for her, but he caught her arm and held her back.

"Anna needed some air and I came back to make sure she was alright. We're coming back in now, so just chill out."

Thankfully, Jake had known Ryan long enough to get it when there was more left unsaid. He nodded and turned to go back inside, leaving them for a few more minutes of privacy. "Got it. Just get back in here, it's getting busy inside and it's damn cold out here."

When the door closed behind him, Anna let out her breath that she had not even realized she was holding. Logically, she understood that Callie had probably told Jake what she knew about Anna's past, but that didn't mean she was ready to admit that she had been so scared by a customer who hadn't even said anything to her. Nervously, she looked up at Ryan. "Thanks for not saying anything about why I ran out. I hope he's not too mad."

"Nah, he's fine. Don't worry about anything, okay? But he is right, it is fucking freezing out here." Ryan rubbed his hands up and down Anna's arms. "Come on, let's get you inside before I decide your kisses are addicting enough for us to really piss off

Jake and go home for the night."

Anna laughed, feeling lighter than she had in a long time. "Oh no, whatever would my boss say to that?"

"Trust me, this boss would love it." With a wink and a grin Ryan tugged her back inside.

8

Chapter 7

Anna slept soundly that night and awoke from a dream of Ryan's strong arms holding her, and his luscious mouth covering her entire body with kisses. He had shown her such kindness and affection last night, she knew it was only a matter of time before she gave in to the feelings building inside her. The way he had managed to soothe her panic and help her find her own strength again was incredible. It was such a gift and Anna wasn't sure he even realized what it meant to her.

A cold nose poked Anna's arm as it lay on top of her quilt, waking her fully from her drowsy thoughts. Samson whined quietly, as Anna stretched and slowly sat up to see sunlight filtering through a gap in her drapes. She reached down to fondle his soft ears, and he looked up at her with eyes that did a poor job of disguising his need for a visit outside.

"Okay, buddy, I get it. Let's go." Anna climbed out of bed and pulled on a pair of warm socks to ward against the early morning chill. She could hear that the furnace had kicked on as it was programmed to do, but this early in the morning, the house was still quite cool.

Anna opened the back door for Samson who took off with a joyous bark to run and sniff around the backyard, before taking care of his business. When he came back inside, she toweled off his feet before she fed him breakfast, then finally went to turn on the coffee machine. As she was about to fill the pot with water, the new cell phone she had purchased yesterday with Ryan chimed with a text message. Her heart thumped with excitement when she saw it was from him.

RYAN: Hey, sweetheart, hope you had a good sleep last night. Let me know if you need anything today.

Touched by his kindness in checking in with her, she responded with what she hoped wasn't too eager a reply.

ANNA: I slept like a log. Just about to make some coffee, maybe we could take Samson for a walk later today? I'd like to see you.

Chewing on her thumb as she waited for his response, Anna anxiously worried she had come on too strongly by asking Ryan to get together today. Just then a gentle knock on the door startled her as another message came through at the same time.

RYAN: **Open up, it's me.**

Flustered, Anna jumped up from the couch, disturbing Samson who was lying across her feet. She nervously ran her hands over her hair, wishing she had time to brush her teeth or put on something other than pajamas and fuzzy socks. Pulling open the front door she saw him standing on her front step, a soft smile on his face, looking as handsome and charming as ever. Two coffee cups were in his hands and he reached one out to her. "Vanilla latte for the lady. I hope it's okay I stopped by, I really wanted to make sure you were doing alright after everything that happened last night. My text was only to see if you were up already, but I figured with Samson you probably were."

Anna felt her heart melt a little more as she realized that not only had he been concerned for how she would be feeling but he had also brought her favorite drink. Fleetingly, she recalled Callie saying Ryan had always been a selfish playboy, but the man in front of her was anything but that. He had shown her nothing but kindness, respect, and affection.

"You're sweet, thank you," she said as she stepped back to let him in, "just give me a minute to get dressed."

Before she could get more than one step away Ryan pulled her back toward him and bent down to press a firm kiss to her lips. "I don't know, I think penguin pajamas are perfect for a cold morning like today."

Any sense of embarrassment over her appearance disappeared under the wave of heat that consumed her with just that simple embrace. Staring up at Ryan's face, Anna was about to kiss him again when she stopped and pulled back in horror. "Ohmygod! I haven't even brushed my teeth! I'll be right back." Then she ran up the stairs before Ryan had a chance to respond.

In the privacy of her bathroom, Anna took in a deep breath. Looking in the mirror she was amazed at the flush of arousal she could see on her face. This man was able to spark feelings in her that had been dormant for a very long time. She touched her lips, lost in the memory of his kiss. The strength, the passion, the gentle security she could feel in his embrace was such a potent aphrodisiac it sent a thrill straight to her core. Suddenly desperate to get back to him, she quickly brushed her teeth and twisted her long brown hair into a simple braid. Deciding not to bother getting dressed, she went back downstairs to find Ryan sitting on her couch, Samson curled up beside him.

"I see someone has made himself comfortable," she teased as she dropped to the couch on the other side of the dog.

Ryan grinned in response. "I swear he just hopped up and gave me these soulful eyes that charmed me. I was powerless to say no."

"I know the feeling." Her breath caught as the words slipped out. She might not have meant to say it now, but it was true and she wouldn't take it back. "You and your eyes have charmed me, Ryan."

* * *

Ryan felt his heart stop at those words and the sincere expression in Anna's beautiful hazel eyes. Reality hit him in that instant. This incredible woman was opening her heart to him. He was suddenly torn in two. He felt on top of the world for earning her trust, but fast on the heels of that high was the crashing low of abject fear at letting her down. How could he ignore his past? Ryan was not a man for relationships, for commitment. The idea of hurting Anna, in any way, had him sick to his stomach. It's not that he was a love 'em and leave 'em guy, hell he was barely a like 'em and leave 'em guy. Ryan simply never let a woman get close enough for any feelings to be involved. So, what the hell was he doing now?

The warm look on Anna's face made it clear she was oblivious to the inner turmoil Ryan had just gone through. So, pushing his thoughts aside, he tried to focus back on the present moment, and the undeniable pull between them. He gently pushed Samson off the couch, before moving closer to Anna.

She was sitting with her feet tucked up underneath her petite body, looking so peaceful and happy it made his heart ache with a longing to see that look on her face all the time. He tucked a stray piece of hair behind her ear, bringing a soft smile to her face.

Unable to hold back, Ryan leaned in and pressed a soft kiss to the side of her face. "Anna, I need to tell you something." He didn't know where the words were coming from, only that they had to break free. "I'm drawn to you, sweetheart. I know you have been through hell, even if I don't yet know exactly what that means. The last thing I want to do is push you too fast, but I can't help it. Something about you feels so right. I can't explain it, hell I've never felt it before, but it's the truth—this just feels right." He took her hands in his. "I need you to know, I don't do relationships, I never have. So, I'm terrified of messing up and hurting you somehow. I'd never want to hurt you, but it might just be in my DNA. The thing is, I know I would feel like an idiot if I didn't at least try to tell you how I feel."

Tears pooled in Anna's eyes, and when one slowly broke free he reached up and brushed it away. He had never been so nervous to hear a woman's response. The happy emotions that played out on her face was all the reassurance he needed to know his feelings were not one sided.

"Don't be terrified. I believe that you will never hurt me on purpose," Anna said as she clasped his hands in her own and pulled them onto her lap. "I'm not very good at relationships either, which is obvious given my track record," she laughed self-deprecatingly, "but I also know I want to try. With you."

Choked with emotion, all Ryan could do to respond was hold her face in his hands. His thumbs brushed her cheeks as they sat there, in silence for a moment. Content to just look at each other with hopeful smiles. Then gently, slowly, Ryan leaned in and pressed his forehead to Anna's and whispered, "That makes me insanely happy to hear."

* * *

Who knew a whisper could hold such heat. Anna's eyes drifted closed as Ryan's lips softly touched each corner of her mouth before settling on the middle. He slowly increased the pressure, and she felt herself opening to him. As their tongues danced together, Anna's hands entwined themselves in Ryan's hair, holding him close. She could feel the scorching touch of his hands running along the side of her body through the thin fabric of her pajama top and was consumed with a yearning to feel his hands on her skin.

As if he was reading her mind, Ryan slowly inched his hands underneath her shirt. At the first brush of his hand against her breast, Anna gasped, breaking their kiss. His hand froze, and she opened her eyes to see Ryan looking intently, worriedly, at her face. What he said next, couldn't have been sweeter.

"Are you okay with this? I meant it when I said I didn't want to push you too fast."

The earnest concern in his voice was like cupid's arrow shooting straight at her heart. She marveled at how this beautiful, sexy man was so focused on her feelings instead of his own needs. Wanting to show him, not just tell him, exactly how okay with everything she was, Anna reached down and pulled her shirt off without a word. There was no mistaking the lustful darkening of Ryan's eyes at the sight of her bare breasts. Desperate not to give in to her nerves, Anna reached over and tugged at the bottom of his shirt. He didn't miss a beat before pulling it over his head, then grabbed Anna and pulled her toward him as he leaned back to recline on the couch, ending with her on top of him, pressing her breasts into his muscular chest.

"You're in control, Anna."

"Then kiss me, Ryan. Kiss me everywhere." Her breathy words took Anna by surprise, but then again, he did take her breath away.

As their mouths crashed together again, Anna's hands ran up and down the ridges of muscle on Ryan's back. His hands were around her waist, all it took was a slight shift in position and suddenly he was grasping her hips and pulling their bodies even closer. She could feel the hard length of his obvious erection straining between her legs, and an answering tingle went straight to her core. A moan escaped her lips, as he trailed kisses along her neck.

In a swift move he flipped them over, so that she lay on the couch cradled between his arms. Her heart was beating so strongly she was certain that he could hear it, but he gave no indication of that when he traveled down her neck to her chest before capturing one of her breasts in his mouth. He gently teased the nipple into a stiff bud, bringing whimpers of pleasure from Anna. She barely recognized the wanton woman she was becoming under his touch.

"God, Anna, I love how your body responds to me." Ryan pressed open-mouthed kisses to the space between her breasts before moving over to the other side and lavishing it with similar attention.

"It's so good. I've never felt this before." She gasped as he gently bit down. "Don't stop. Please don't stop!" Anna moaned at the sensations coursing through her. Her eyes fluttered closed as he moved down her torso, reaching down to slide her pants down her legs. Her hands found his head and twisted in his hair, holding him to her.

"I need to taste you, Anna. Please let me."

Ryan's voice held a desperate, pleading note that Anna had never heard from him before. Unable to formulate words to express just how much she wanted that, she let her legs fall open beneath him, telling him with her body how ready she was. When the cool air of the morning hit her naked body, she sucked in a breath at the feel of him nuzzling her inner thighs.

She should have been embarrassed. Anna was far from a virgin, but she had never let another man be this intimate with her. She could count the number of orgasms she had experienced in her life on one hand, and she'd never felt like a sensual woman before. Yet here and now, under Ryan's touch, she came alive with erotic pleasure.

When his tongue stroked her folds with its wet heat, her hips lifted off the couch as she screamed at the tantalizing sensation. Ryan's strong hands wrapped around her hips to hold her in place as he tasted and teased her, whipping her into a frenzy. His tongue darted in and out, caressing her in a way that was new and wonderful. It seemed like mere seconds before she was cascading into an intense orgasm. He continued to suck and kiss her core, soothing it as she came down from the high, before slowly working his way back up her body, and stretching out beside her. When Anna opened her eyes at last, Ryan was leaning over her, a satisfied grin on his face as his fingers lazily stroked up and down her side.

"Yes, ma'am, you are welcome," he said with a wink, eliciting a laugh from deep within Anna's heart. This man had just brought her higher than she had ever been, had held her as she all too rapidly crashed over the edge of pleasure, and now was making her smile and relax just as quickly.

"You're ridiculous," she teased, reaching up to caress his

face.

"Nah, just really invested in your happiness. Making you smile, making you laugh, making you orgasm, those are pretty much my top three favorite things to do now."

"I'm not complaining about that list at all."

Ryan leaned down to nuzzle Anna's neck. "Can we move this into your bedroom, sweetheart? As much as I want to claim you on every goddamn surface in this place, you deserve to have our first time be a little more special."

Anna pushed at his naked chest, and they both rose off the couch. As she took his hand to walk up the stairs toward her bedroom, she turned and looked over her shoulder coyly, embracing her newfound confidence, infusing her voice with it. "You're sounding pretty romantic for someone who doesn't do relationships..."

Anna regretted the words as soon as they came out. Even though she meant them teasingly, she didn't miss the slight flash of pain in Ryan's eyes. Before she could take back what she said, the pain was gone. With a devilish grin he tugged her back against his chest, wrapping his arms around her bare stomach, his fingers dancing dangerously close to her still wet core.

"What can I say, you inspire me to change."

The pang in Anna's heart was sudden and unexpected, as she realized how desperately she wanted that to be true. She honestly believed that Ryan would never intentionally hurt her, but she also wasn't fool enough to believe a playboy could be reformed just like that. However, knowing that still didn't ease the longing deep inside.

9

Chapter 8

Ryan could barely keep his desire in check as Anna's naked body swayed in front of him. His hands and mouth burned to taste and feel every inch of her. But alongside his desire was the doubt born of his longstanding doubts about love and relationships. He vehemently wished he could break free of the fears and insecurities inside his mind. He wanted nothing more than to quiet the insidious voice that warned him away from love, away from commitment. The voice that sounded so much like his dad.

For a man who was barely around during Ryan's childhood, he'd certainly left his share of scars. Ryan had seen enough pictures to know how similar he was in appearance to his father. He had heard enough stories of the legendary Carlisle charm, to recognize that his own behaviors around women likely mirrored those of the man who had contributed half of his DNA. The fear of hurting someone the way his father had hurt his mother was enough to keep Ryan running far and fast from any sort of real relationship with a woman. His friendships with Callie and Reagan were the only meaningful connections he had formed with a woman, other than his mother, in his entire adult life. And now, one woman was rewriting every definition, every belief he ever had of himself.

Anna with her lustrous hair that was soft as silk in his hands. Anna with her moans of pleasure. Anna who had dug her way deep into his heart so quickly he had not realized she was there until now. For her, he wanted to be romantic. He wanted to be in a relationship. But damn, was he terrified of hurting her.

Pushing away these consuming thoughts, Ryan forced himself back into the present. He stood in Anna's bedroom, watching her delicate movements, confident in her nudity, as she turned on a soft light and pulled the blinds closed. The bleary morning outside faded into a warm cocoon. He could smell the fragrance he had begun to associate with her, a soft citrusy scent.

Ryan unbuttoned his jeans, pulled out the condom he had stashed there earlier and placed it on the bedside table. When Anna turned toward him, he was gratified to hear her breath catch at the sight of his naked body. He knew his erection was jutting out proudly, seeking her heat. Ryan was determined not to rush things. He wanted to cherish Anna, make her feel safe and ensure she found her release before he took his own. That didn't stop the raging fire inside of him that shouted for him to just fucking claim the woman in front of him. *Tame the beast...* Those words that Jake had spoken weeks ago came back to Ryan in that moment. Never had the statement been truer than in this instant. Anna was taming him. And he didn't mind at all.

He walked toward her, gently pushing her backward until her legs hit the bed, and she sat down. The gruffness in his voice was foreign to him, laced with emotion. "Lay back, sweetheart."

She did as he asked, and the sight of her shiny hair spread across the pale duvet just about broke the thin thread of control he was holding onto. He crawled up her body before settling in between her legs. The hot moisture of her sex coated his cock, making it throb with desire.

Sliding his fingers down her stomach, he dipped them between her soft, slick folds. "You're so ready for me. It drives me fucking crazy." He bent down and grazed Anna's nipple with his teeth, causing her to arch up into his mouth. A satisfied growl came from deep within at the sound of her shuddering breath of pleasure. His fingers slid in and out of her wet heat as his thumb grazed her clit.

"Ryan!"

Anna's gasp as he flicked her clit was so damn hot, he had to do it again. Her hands roamed his back, her nails digging in occasionally as he explored her, learning just what sent her flying. But he held back this time, pulling his fingers free when he felt her start to clench around him.

"The next time you come, it needs to be around my cock. Call me selfish but I need to feel you."

"I want that, please. I need that now."

Anna's voice was filled with arousal and he drank in the rapture on her face as she watched him sheath his cock in protection. He stretched out over her, the heat of their bodies pressed together. Then slowly, ever so slowly, he lined up with her center and began to press his way in. Watching Anna's face carefully, Ryan levered himself up so he could control his movements. Who knew how long it had been since she had been treated with compassion and intimacy. He was determined to make this experience special for her.

As he worked his length inside of her, he began a slow but steady rhythmic thrust. The base of his cock slid against her swollen clit with every slide, eliciting a gasp from Anna. Her upturned face was the picture of blissful beauty as he leaned over to cover her with soft kisses. When she pulled her legs up to wrap them around his torso, he felt the responding clench of her channel.

"Oh god I'm close. So close," she moaned.

"Just let go. I'm right there with you."

With just those words, he could feel Anna tighten around his cock, and when she let out a scream of release, he slowed his movement, riding out her orgasm, holding back from his own. He had never exercised such restraint in bed before and had to admit that the inferno building inside him was worth the wait.

When at last Anna's eyes opened, with a dreamy, satisfied look in them, his ego roared with satisfaction. She pulled his head down for a kiss, their tongues tangling with passion. He slowly started to move again, bringing another moan from her lips. Holding her close, he rolled, bringing Anna on top of his body without losing contact where it mattered most.

Anna, straddling his cock, had to be the single most perfect view he had ever seen. Her lips were swollen from their kisses, her hair flowed down over her shoulders in a cascade. Ryan found himself frozen, captivated by her beauty and by the intimacy of the moment.

"Damn, you're beautiful. This... This feels... This is everything," he stuttered, embarrassed at how close he had come to professing feelings he was not even sure he was capable of having.

Thankfully, Anna didn't seem to notice his almost admission. She smiled down at him, before beginning to slowly rock her hips back and forth, bringing his still-hard cock right back to attention. He marveled at how open and free she was. Gone was the nervous woman who had walked into his bar, and in her place was a seductive siren who was confidently taking what she needed if her sounds of pleasure were any indication. As their movements sped up, he began thrusting deeper into Anna's core, reveling in how tightly she held him inside. With a groan he reached between them to play with her clit, rewarded by a gasp as she fell forward, her hands landing on his chest, her hair tickling his nipples.

"How are you... I can't believe I'm going to... Again... Ryan!"

His name came out as a scream as Anna let go in another spectacular release that sent him rushing off the edge into his own orgasm after her. When she eventually collapsed onto his chest, their bodies clung together with sweat. Ryan stroked Anna's back, reveling in the feel of their heartbeats racing together. He had never experienced sex that was more than just sex. What had happened just now was so much more; it was the coming together of two souls. Never in his life had sex left him wanting more than just a physical connection. It wasn't just that he wanted that with Anna, he was beginning to realize he needed it. Like a man coming out of the desert needed water.

* * *

Slowly, Anna forced her breathing back to a normal rate. Her head spun with the overwhelming sensations from multiple earth-shattering orgasms. Ryan had touched—literally and figuratively—parts of her body and soul she had thought would never feel again after her time with Tim. Being with Ryan had woken a sensual side to her, a side she very much enjoyed. And he had managed to do all of that, with the utmost care and concern for her own pleasure and comfort before his own.

Gradually they moved so they were lying side by side. Ryan had pulled Anna in close, and she nestled her head on his shoulder, enjoying his masculine aroma, tinged with the musky scent of their release. She sighed, before pressing a kiss to his neck, tasting the faint saltiness of his sweat. Anna waited for her nerves to kick in, for the feelings of self-consciousness she had lived with for two years to come roaring back. But with the feel of Ryan's hands holding her tight, there was no room for doubt. She felt protected, adored, wanted. Looking up at him, she reached a hand up to brush a lock of hair off his forehead. He smiled in response, a satisfied, happy smile.

With a blush, Anna blurted out, "Thank you seems like such a stupid thing to say right now."

"From my perspective, thank you sounds pretty good, sweetheart. Thank you for blowing my mind. Thank you for trusting me with your gorgeous body. Thank you for letting me in and giving me a chance."

Once again, Ryan's romantic words left Anna awestruck. How could this man say he was terrible at relationships yet be so charming? Overcome with her attraction to him, she buried her head back into his shoulder. Gradually she felt her body relax. They lay there in a peaceful silence for several minutes. The only sound was the gentle tick tock of the old-fashioned clock Aunt Theresa had given Anna years ago. Having Ryan in her childhood home felt oddly comfortable. As if he was meant to be there all along.

Before she could make sense of that idea, Ryan shifted slightly so that he could prop up on his elbow and look down at her. "So, what did you have planned for today? I know you've got the night off, and I don't have to be at my mom's house until later, so can we do something together?"

A wicked smile crept over Anna's face, and before she could overthink her flirtatious reply, she let it out, "I thought we DID just do something together..."

Ryan let out a laugh that started her giggling as well. "We certainly did. And trust me, I would like to do that with you again very soon." Ryan's tone sobered. "But if you're going to give me a chance, then I want to do this relationship thing right. Which means I want to take you out for a day-date."

"A day-date?"

"Yeah. A daytime date. Maybe not as romantic as an evening date but with both of us working at The Lucky Strike, day-dates might be the best we can do sometimes. I hope that's okay."

Anna smiled. "That sounds absolutely wonderful. Can our day-date include Samson? He needs some exercise."

As if on cue, there was a scratch at the bedroom door and Samson let out a whine. Ryan leaned down and kissed Anna. "I think that's a fantastic idea."

10

Chapter 9

Bundled up against the cold, with fresh cups of coffee in hand, they headed out for a walk. As they passed a snow-covered playing field, Ryan gave Anna a boyish smile before he handed her his coffee and took off running with Samson through the snow. The dog barked in delight as Ryan played with him, tossing snowballs, and chasing him around in circles. Anna stood to the side taking it all in. She had never expected to find such happiness when she returned to Portland. Her only thoughts had been about escaping Tim, trying to put enough distance between them, and desperately wanting to start over. Yet here she was, with a man who'd made her experience more joy in the last twenty-four hours than she had thought possible. For the first time in a long time, she felt safe, cared for, and excited for what might come next.

Anna laughed at the sight of Ryan, looking incredibly sexy in his jeans, hoodie and down vest, running after Samson. His nose was red, his eyes bright with energy and joy as man and dog raced around. Ryan's natural athleticism was evident in his quick maneuvers and sheer speed.

As she watched Samson leap around Ryan's legs in sheer delight, Anna noticed some kids arrive with a soccer ball. They kicked it around for a moment, until it rolled over to Ryan. She was amazed to see him kick the ball up in the air with some fancy footwork, bouncing it easily between his feet even on the slippery, snowy ground. *He looks like a professional...*

She was too far away to hear his words, but watched as he brought the ball back to the kids. They were animated in whatever they said to him, as he first gestured to her, then seemed to agree to whatever they had asked. Anna wandered over to see what was going on, just in time to hear the kids and Ryan laugh as he tried to teach them some tricks with the ball. She clipped Samson on to his leash and hung back, content to watch Ryan in his element, playing soccer with some kids.

After a while, Ryan said goodbye to the kids, with fist bumps and high fives all around. He came over to Anna and slung his arm over her shoulder before pressing a loud kiss to the side of her head.

"Sorry about that, but those kids—man, they were fun," he said.

Anna looked up at the exhilaration on Ryan's face. "It's no problem. They were loving every minute. You're incredible to watch with a soccer ball!"

A rueful look came into Ryan's eyes. "Yeah, well, soccer has always been my real passion in life. I love messing around with a ball."

Before Anna could ask him why he was running a bar instead of following his passion, she remembered what he had said on their walk around downtown. Something had made Ryan give up his dream. She opened her mouth to try and get him to tell her more, but Ryan changed direction, and pulled her toward some low buildings at the end of the field.

"Come on, sweetheart. Let me take you out to lunch. This place has the best Reuben you've ever had, and they're dog friendly so Samson can come inside."

Aware that he didn't seem inclined to talk any more about soccer, Anna let it go—for now. Still, she knew all too well what it felt like to abandon your dreams. Then and there she decided to try and help Ryan somehow find his way back to soccer. After all, he was helping her find her joy again, why could she not try to do the same for him?

* * *

"Wow, you weren't exaggerating; this sandwich is incredible. How did you find this place?"

"I've always liked the smaller places, the restaurants that feel like home. That's what Jake and I tried to create at The Lucky Strike. A place that was just chill and relaxed." Ryan shrugged modestly.

"You've certainly done that, the bar is amazing and obviously people love it." Anna's budding curiosity could no longer be contained, but she knew she had to tread lightly. "What made you decide to open a bar in the first place?"

Settling back in his chair, a wistful smile crept over Ryan's face and his eyes grew distant, as he lost himself in memories. "Ah, that's quite the story. I never imagined I would be my own boss that's for damn sure. The only reason I have the career, the life, I have now is because of Jake. He helped me find a way out of a shitty situation. He's my best friend, my partner, hell, pretty much my savior. You remember I told you the other day, I had to give up my dream?" Anna nodded. "I guess it's time you heard the whole story. I met Jake in our first year of college. I was there on a soccer scholarship, headed for the major leagues—or so I thought. We ended up as roommates in the freshmen dorms. He was a cool guy, so it was easy to become buddies. We ruled that dorm."

Ryan paused, took a drink of water and chuckled. "Those were the days. I was playing soccer and skating through easy classes; Jake was busting his ass in business school. Our nights were filled with parties, girls, and nothing but good times. We had our goals, and nothing was going to stand in our way. We thought we were fucking untouchable."

Anna leaned forward, eager to hear more. Somehow, she understood she was getting a glimpse into Ryan's past that not many people knew. His bravado and playful attitude hid layers of emotion and pain, that she was now starting to see.

"Then one day, one stupid rainy day my junior year, everything changed." Ryan was silent for a moment before he went on in a low voice. "The field was muddy and slippery. It was just a regular practice, but my teammate and I collided at just the wrong angle. He was moving to kick the ball and kicked my knee instead. The doc said I blew all the ligaments so completely, there would be no coming back even with surgery. The knee would never be stable enough to play at the level I was headed for."

Anna's heart broke at the pain evident in Ryan's voice. She ached with wanting to hold him; to take away his sorrow both now, and back then as a young man devastated by the painful end to his dreams.

At a loss as to what words could possibly provide comfort, she gave in to her instincts and went around the table before sitting down in his lap. If the look of surprise on his face was any indication, it was the right move.

She tried to inject some lightness into the mood. "I'm sure you were one sexy soccer player, but if it's any consolation... you're pretty hot behind a bar too."

Anna pressed her lips to his, in what was intended to be a sweet, flirtatious kiss. It was only a second before Ryan's arms tightened around her waist, and he deepened the embrace into something far more heated. Behind the heat, was a desperation that she could feel bleeding through. A desperation for support, for comfort, maybe even for love?

As soon as that thought hit her, she pulled back. Love? No way, she wasn't ready for that. And Ryan himself had always said he didn't do relationships, and love certainly meant a relationship. No, she needed to move away from the L word immediately. Even if the idea of letting herself fully commit to Ryan, and having him fully commit to her, was extremely enticing.

Determined to keep the conversation going, and to force her own thoughts to move on, she asked, "So, tell me more. How did you go from soccer star to sexiest bartender alive?"

Ryan's arms were rigid around her waist, anchoring her in place. It was as if he unconsciously needed her near him to get through whatever he was about to say.

"After my knee went, I hit a bad place. Without soccer, there was nothing in my life to give me structure, or meaning, or fuck, even an identity. Who was I if I wasn't Ryan Carlisle the soccer star? I was lost. I pulled away from everyone. Dropped out of school, ignored my mom and my brother for weeks. Jake was living off campus by then and he let me crash on his couch. There were days where I didn't even bother getting dressed. I was seriously fucked up." Ryan winced, looking at Anna sheepishly. "Sorry, Anna. I know this isn't exactly giving you the best impression of me. It's way too soon, in whatever this is between us, for me to be telling you all about my crazy breakdown."

Anna grabbed his face, forcing his gaze to hers. "Now you listen to me. Your feelings and your experiences do not make you crazy. There is absolutely nothing wrong with my impression of you. Got it?" She pressed a firm kiss to his lips again, trying to cement her words into his mind. "Now keep going. You hit rock bottom at some point obviously, and Jake helped?"

Ryan looked at her in wonder. "You just keep on surprising me. Damn you have a big heart. Yeah, after a few months I was a mess. Hungover most days, and let me tell you the hangover from alcohol and painkillers? Not fun. I knew I needed to figure my life out but had no clue what to do next. Anyway, Jake was working on this assignment for school. A business plan, and he made his for a brew pub. His grandfather encouraged him to make the pub a reality, and somehow Jake convinced me to join him. Honestly, I think he asked me during that time of my hangover I would agree to any wild idea. We started to spend our nights dreaming up plans for the pub. We decided I would take the lead on the bartending, so I threw myself into that. Took all kinds of classes, studied up on different drinks, Jake and I even took some beer making courses just in case we ever decided to have our own custom brew. He convinced me to join him bartending at a place on campus. I fucking loved being around people again. The energy, the... ah, female attention..."

Ryan had the decency to look embarrassed by that statement. Anna just smiled and nodded at him to continue.

"The crucial part for me was, if I showed up to work drunk or hungover, I got in shit. The boss was a hardass, but a fair one. Kind of like my soccer coach. Finally, I had the structure I needed, and a goal. That helped me turn things around and the rest is history."

Still seated in his lap, without a care to what anyone else in the diner might be thinking, Anna laid her head on Ryan's shoulder. "I am truly sorry you had to give up your dream..." Anna hesitated, unsure if what she was about to say would be too much. "But a part of me is selfishly happy. If you were playing soccer right now, instead of working at the pub, we never would have met. You have changed my life, Ryan. You are helping me find my way out of a really dark place, just like Jake did for you. For that, I'll always be grateful."

* * *

The solemn tone of Anna's voice held Ryan in place. She was right, without his knee injury, he never would have started the bar with Jake, and he never would have met Anna. Suddenly he was faced with the realization that what had always been the darkest part of his life, might actually have a silver lining. But closing in fast on the heels of that thought came all his familiar worries. Was he too much like his dad to ever love a woman without causing them pain? Could he take the risk of hurting Anna, just because he selfishly wanted to be with her? In that instant Ryan knew he had to tell her everything. He had shared so much, more than he ever had with anyone outside of his family and Jake. Anna deserved it all, especially if there was to be any hope of a future.

"Anna, you need to know that telling you all of this today was not exactly what I had planned. Hell, I never thought I would let myself get close enough to anyone to tell them about my past. You're special sweetheart. This, what we have, is special." He took in a deep breath and encouraged by the smile spreading over her face continued, "Which is why I'm scared shitless. When I said I don't do relationships, I meant it. I never thought I would let myself fall for someone, because I knew I would hurt them eventually."

The soft touch of Anna's hand on his face almost broke his resolve to finish. He could tell she wanted to interrupt, so he forged on through and said, "My entire life I've heard how much I look like my dad and my grandfather. The stories about the *Irish charm* of the Carlisle men were so ingrained in me, that when I was old enough to be interested in girls, I figured I had to live up to the name. I was such a jerk to girls. The problem is, I also grew up seeing the shitty side of that charm. I watched my dad cheat on my mom so many times. He'd yell at her for some random reason, storm out, and then come back the next day smelling of stale perfume. For years, my mom put up with it. Then, when I was ten, he left for good and didn't come back."

Ryan shifted in his seat, but kept his arms around Anna. She was his anchor, the only reason he could find the courage to voice the fears that had held him back from love his entire life. "It was better after he left. But Mom was stuck trying to raise two wild boys on her own, as well as deal with the breakdown of her shitty marriage. There were so many nights I could hear her crying herself to sleep. She would look at me sometimes, and I would see the pain she felt seeing my dad reflected back at her. Then, when I was a sixteen-year-old dumbass, I stood up my girlfriend on our one-month anniversary to go and play soccer with some guys. I thought nothing of it until the next day when all her friends yelled at me during lunch. When I realized that even a stupid teenage romance could hurt, I decided never to commit to a woman again. Keep it casual, make that clear from the beginning, and no one can get hurt."

A weight lifted from Ryan's shoulders just by finally saying those words to someone. Still, before he could let Anna reply, there was one more thing he had to say. "Here's the thing, Anna. You came along, out of nowhere, and turned everything I believed upside down. Suddenly I want a relationship, with you. I'm just so scared I'll hurt you." When he finished, Ryan found himself overcome with nerves. How would she react?

The silence stretched between them, as he searched Anna's face for some idea of how she was feeling. Anna was looking down at their laps, her lower lip pulled between her teeth. He desperately wanted to tug it free and kiss her, just to feel their physical connection holding strong.

After what felt like eternity, she looked up at him. Her eyes held a look of concern, but Ryan was hopeful that what he saw glimmering in their depths was a desire to be together.

"I didn't come to Portland looking for a relationship. I was escaping one. You know I have been hurt before, I don't want to be hurt again," she said softly.

Ryan's heart dropped at Anna's words. He started to move away, to let her get off his lap and leave. But she surprised him by wrapping her arms around his shoulders, pulling him back into their embrace.

"I'm not finished, Ryan, so wipe that mopey look off your face."

Her voice was so fierce, it was adorable. Ryan smiled as hope began to bloom.

Keeping her eyes on his, she went on, "Here's the thing. You think that you are no good at relationships, but that's not what you've shown me. These past few weeks you have been romantic, protective, caring, and respectful—all the qualities I would want in a boyfriend. I don't want to be hurt, and I don't think you will hurt me. So, like I said yesterday, I'm in if you're in."

Ryan grinned. He had told her everything. All the dark pieces of his past were laid out in front of Anna, and she still wanted to be with him. He pulled her toward him and crushed her mouth to his. Pouring his feeling into the kiss, he vowed to himself that he would do every damn thing possible to never let Anna be hurt by himself, or anyone else, ever again.

* * *

Reluctant to leave each other's side after the emotions shared between them, Anna and Ryan slowly wandered back to her house after lunch. There they had to part ways for the evening, as Anna was going to her neighbor's house to hear more about her Aunt Theresa, and Ryan had plans with his mom and brother.

As he stood on Anna's steps, Ryan simply stared at her for a moment. This incredible woman was rewriting every negative belief he had ever held about himself. Even so, the force of her kindness and understanding didn't quite erase all of his fears and doubts that he would one day hurt her. He knew she sensed his hesitation when he saw the curious and—damn it—guarded look in her eyes. This was what he was worried about. Anna was already doubting him, doubting his ability to fully be in this relationship. He cursed to himself, angry that he might have revealed too much, too soon.

"Sweetheart, I..."

"Ryan..."

They both laughed awkwardly. Ryan gestured for Anna to continue.

"Ryan, it means so much to me that you trusted me enough to tell me everything. I honestly don't believe you would ever hurt me on purpose, but I can see you're still nervous. No amount of words I say will convince you that this can work. I don't want to deny what's between us, but maybe we should take things more slowly."

His heart plummeted at her words. But he knew she was right. He was still nervous, so rushing headlong into his first serious relationship probably wasn't a wise choice. Especially not with someone as important to him as Anna had quickly become. Breathing deeply to slow his racing thoughts, he tried to respond.

"I understand. I really don't want to mess this up. I'm not going anywhere, but if you want to go slowly, we will. Please don't give up on me, okay?" He was embarrassed by the pleading sound of his voice, but knew he was speaking from his heart.

"Of course I won't, silly." Anna cupped his cheeks, smiling up at him. "And slowing down doesn't mean moving backward. So, any time you want to repeat this morning's fun... Well, you know where to find me."

Ryan groaned at the thought of Anna writhing in bed beneath him, and growled in response. "Fuck, Anna, you have no idea how much I want to do that right now. If I wasn't worried that your neighbor was peeking through her curtains next door waiting for me to leave, I'd take you right here right now."

Anna laughed, then squirmed as Ryan pressed her into his body, showing her just how ready he was to make good on his offer. Her gasp at the feel of his hard cock between them was just what he hoped to hear. Kissing her firmly on the lips, he pulled away before he let things go too far.

"I'll see you soon, Anna."

Then he turned around and walked quickly to his truck, not daring to look back and be tempted by her face, which he knew would be flushed with arousal. As it was, he struggled to adjust his hard-on when he sat in his truck, and had to settle for hoping it would die down before he got to his mom's house.

This woman was bewitching him, that was for sure.

* * *

Dinner at Molly Carlisle's house was an informal affair. As a single mother of two rambunctious boys, she had long ago given up on things like fancy china and elegant meals. So much time had been spent driving to different sports, helping with homework, and working long hours to keep her bank account from going too far into the red.

Even now, with Ryan and Noah grown and living their own lives, Molly kept things simple. A big pan of tuna casserole was always a hit, and tonight both men dug in with gusto. After everyone had eaten, Molly turned to Ryan. "Honey, how are things going at the pub? Were you and Jake able to hire some more staff?"

How his mom managed to remember every detail of what was happening in their lives, Ryan would never know. But her memory, and how she cared about mundane things like staffing, was deeply appreciated by her boys.

"Yeah, we were, Mom. Things are good now. Busy still, but with the extra help we're doing okay."

"I heard a rumor that the new help is pretty hot... and maybe doing more with you than just working at the bar," Noah said teasingly.

Ryan's older brother often worked out at the same gym as Ryan and Jake, so it was no surprise he had heard about Anna.

"Shut up, asshole," Ryan shot back with a punch to Noah's arm.

"Boys, stop." Molly held her hands up, and just as it had when they were kids, her commanding voice made both men freeze. "Now, Ryan. What is Noah talking about? Are you dating one of your staff? Honey, that's not a good idea." She looked at him with concern.

"It's not like that at all, Mom." Ryan quickly jumped to defend his relationship, "Yeah, Anna works at the pub, but it's okay, trust me. Jake is cool with it."

"Hmmm, alright, just be careful." Molly wiped her hands with her napkin before settling back in her chair, her gaze turning from concerned to openly curious. "Tell me about this girl. If she has managed to hold my son's interest, then she must be something special."

Ryan could feel a goofy smile slide across his face just thinking about Anna.

"She is, Mom, she really is. Anna's beautiful, smart, kind, funny. She's just... Yeah. She's special," he said, then noticed his mom and brother were looking at him with surprise. It was his brother, who had always been the more romantic one of the two, that answered first.

"Dude, I've never heard you talk about a girl like that before. Damn, you're in love!"

"No way. I don't do love."

As soon as Ryan said the words, he felt a sharp pang in his chest, as if his heart knew he was lying. But how could he love Anna? It had only been a few weeks, and he had never fallen in love before.

"Oh, honey, you don't still believe that do you?" It was his mother's lovingly concerned voice that shook him out of the swirling tornado that had taken root in Ryan's heart and mind as he tried to process the possibility that he was falling in love with Anna.

"Well, yeah, I do, Mom. I can't be in love with her, or anyone. I can't take the risk of hurting them like Dad hurt you." Ryan winced. He knew any reminder of his father was painful for his mother. He was surprised therefore when she rolled her eyes and scoffed at him.

"Ryan Carlisle, stop being an idiot. You are nothing like your father. Fine, you inherited his good looks and the Carlisle charm, but what you didn't inherit were his loose morals and inability to care about anyone aside from himself." Molly had fire in her eyes as she looked first at Ryan, then at Noah. "Don't you think I deserve some credit? I raised the two of you to respect women, to be considerate of others, and to be hardworking, kind men. I'd like to think I succeeded in that. But if you are telling me that you've held back from love because of some ridiculous notion that you're destined to be a womanizing ass like your father, then maybe I've failed you."

Whether it was the fact that his mother had used a swear word, or the sharpness of her look as she dared either of them to disagree, Ryan and Noah were both frozen in shock at their mother's words.

Noah recovered faster, and quickly tried to placate her. "Don't worry, Mom, I haven't given up on love like this stupid brother of mine. Marriage and kids don't scare me, it's what I've always wanted. I'll make you a grandma, someday."

Then he quickly stood up to clear the table, giving Ryan a meaningful look over his mother's head. A look that clearly implied, *fix this—now.*

Molly sat there, arms folded in front of her, staring at her younger son. After a moment, she sighed, and moved into the chair next to Ryan. Taking his hand, she spoke, softer this time, "Honey, I am so sorry if I've ever said or done anything to make you believe you're like your father. Please believe me, you are not. You are kind and funny and most importantly respectful. Yes, you are also handsome and charming like he was, but I know your heart. And that heart is good and deserves to love a woman just as wonderful as you are. So please, stop letting my mistakes hold you back. Your father was many things, most of them terrible. But he also gave me you and Noah. For that, I don't regret a single thing about my marriage. Open your heart to love, my darling son. If this Anna is half as wonderful as I think she might be, then let her in."

Ryan stayed in his seat for several minutes after that. His mother got up and went into the kitchen to clean up with Noah, leaving Ryan with space to think about what had been said.

Later, they carried on with their evening together, and didn't mention Anna, love, or their father again.

On the drive home, his mother's words bounced around Ryan's mind as he tried to make sense of everything. Hearing her say she didn't regret being with his father, and that she believed Ryan was nothing like him, healed a wound he hadn't realized was there. Slowly, he began to allow himself to imagine a future with Anna. A future not bound by fear that someday he would screw up and destroy what they had. A future where he could happily be in love.

11

Chapter 10

RYAN: I miss you. Twenty-four hours without your sexy body in my arms is way too long.

ANNA: It feels like torture... But a little time apart is good too. Make sure this is what you really want.

Ryan frowned at Anna's text. What the hell did she mean time apart is good? Time apart was terrible. It led to constant obsessing about Anna, and about his feelings. He was not used to this new level of emotional awareness, and it seemed the only time he could quiet the doubts in his mind was when she was in his arms. *Not exactly healthy if she's the only thing keeping you from being a crazy person.* He grimaced, but it wasn't as if he could stop his feelings from happening. At least that was the excuse he gave himself when he decided he was done with only connecting over text messages and pocketed his phone before turning to Jake who was reviewing the last month's numbers with him.

"Look, dude, I know we need to go over this, but I want to go and pick up Anna for her shift."

Jake looked up in surprise. "Seriously? Come on, man, we

need to finish this."

"I know we do." Ryan let out an exasperated sigh. "I get that you're probably pissed, but I have to see her. These fucking feelings are messing with me."

A knowing look came over his friend's face as Jake pushed back from his desk and folded his arms across his chest. With an arrogant smirk he nodded. "Yeah, yeah, go. But the next time you try to give me a hard time for acting sweet around Callie I'll remind you of this."

Not caring how immature his response was, Ryan simply gave Jake the middle finger as he pulled on his jacket and headed out.

Once he was in his truck, driving on autopilot toward Anna's house, Ryan started to wonder if he would be welcome there unannounced. Maybe she was having second thoughts about being with him... Was that why she said time apart could be good? Was he making a mistake ignoring her wishes like this? What if his mom was bullshitting him and he really was destined to be an asshole to women? He could never live with himself if he disrespected Anna.

Ryan was so lost in his spiraling negative thoughts he didn't realize he had pulled into Anna's driveway until he heard a dog bark. Looking up he saw Anna standing on her porch, a curious yet inviting smile on her beautiful face. He quickly jumped out of the truck, giving Samson a quick pat on the head before he walked up to the house.

"Hey, I hope you aren't upset that I just showed up. I just, ah, really wanted to see you."

Ryan jingled his keys in his hand, suddenly overcome with nerves. He was not used to feeling insecure, especially not around women, but Anna was different. She meant so much more to him, which meant the stakes were that much higher. Trying to hold on to his mom's reassurance that he was nothing like his dad, he stopped at the bottom of the steps to the porch. He needed her to make the first move. Her smile went a long way toward making Ryan feel better, but when she skipped down the steps and threw her arms around his neck, he felt a weight lift off his shoulders.

"Of course I'm not upset, silly, I'm happy you're here. Honestly, I thought I was going crazy missing you after only two days." She drew back, searching his face for answers to an unknown question. "But I meant what I said in my text. If some time apart helps you to feel certain that you want to be with me, then I'll survive."

Ryan smiled fondly down at her. "You might survive, but I don't know if I would. If you want me, even knowing about my dad, then I'm all in. I told you I might not be very good at this, but I'm hoping you'll help me."

Ryan hoped she could hear how earnest he was. He truly wanted to make things work with Anna. He just didn't know if he could.

"I'll help you, Ryan. I don't think you need me to, but I promise I will." With that, Anna pressed a sweet kiss to his lips, removing any further doubts—for the moment.

"Now, are you here to give me a ride to work? My boss hates it when I'm late." With a wink, Anna pulled her coat on, put Samson inside and locked the door before walking down toward the truck. A smile crept across Ryan's face. Yes, this woman was worth facing his fears for.

* * *

That night The Lucky Strike was packed with exuberant customers, Ryan was busy pouring drinks all night long, Jake had even stepped behind the bar to help several times. Anna was out front working hard along with two other servers. The busy bar didn't stop Ryan from flirting with her every chance he could. She felt the sparks fly between them with every touch, every smile. Anna didn't dwell on whether it was appropriate for him to behave that way at work, figuring since Jake knew they were together, and he was in charge, it must be alright.

Everything changed, when she dropped off drinks at one of her tables and paused in the back hallway for a moment of rest. Tracy, one of the other servers walked up to her with a judgmental glint in her eyes. Anna didn't know much about the other woman but had seen the flirtatious glances she often gave Ryan, so had her suspicions that Tracy was attracted to him. Standing up straight, Anna tried to steel herself for the attack she instinctively knew was coming.

"I have to say, I'm surprised. Ryan doesn't normally lower himself to sleep with staff, he prefers the drunk bimbos that come in here each night and throw themselves at him. What makes you special? You must have been one hell of a good fuck for him to have given you a job."

Anna was frozen by the horrible things Tracy implied about Ryan and their relationship, as well as by her cruel tone. Before she could gather her thoughts to form a response, Tracy's name was called by someone at the bar. She rolled her eyes at Anna before she stalked off down the hall. Anna sagged against the wall, blindsided by what Tracy had said. She knew that her job was in no way a result of her romantic relationship with Ryan. Yet she wondered if Tracy's obvious displeasure was a sign of a bigger problem. Was she fooling herself to think it was okay for them to be together, especially at work?

As Anna's thoughts sent her careening into despair, Jake stepped out of his office. Embarrassment flooded Anna's mind as she realized he must have heard everything. He beckoned her into his office and closed the door. Fidgeting with her hands, Anna wondered what Jake would say.

"Anna, are you alright?" Concern was evident in Jake's voice, and when she looked up, she didn't see criticism on his face, just friendly compassion. "I heard what she said. I want you to know she was totally out of line. Tracy has wanted to hook up with Ryan ever since she started working here. He's turned her down repeatedly, I guess she doesn't like that. I'm sorry she took it out on you."

A wave of relief crashed over Anna, instantly followed by regret. It was irresponsible of her to flaunt their relationship at work. It didn't matter if Ryan didn't seem to think it was a big deal, he was still technically one of her bosses, and it was totally inappropriate for them to be flirting and touching each other.

"Thanks, Jake, but I'm the one who should apologize. We should have never— "

Jake put his hand up to stop her talking. "Anna, it's fine, you haven't done anything wrong. Yeah, I guess some people might think it isn't cool that Ryan is your boyfriend and boss, but he isn't really in charge, I am." Jake winked. "And, we all know you aren't taking advantage of him or anything. Most importantly he's happy, so I'm happy. I hope you know that you would have a job here no matter what happened between you and Ryan."

He walked over and put his arm loosely on Anna's shoulders. "Now, what should we do about Tracy? We don't tolerate disrespect here, and she had no right to speak to you in that way. I don't want to fire her, that seems a bit over the top, but I do think Ryan and I need to talk to her about her behavior and make sure she understands that your personal life, and Ryan's, is none of her goddamn business. You okay with that?"

Anna was left momentarily speechless by the way Jake had instantly come to her support and alleviated her discomfort over her relationship with Ryan. When she had gathered her thoughts, she looked at Jake who waited patiently for her response. "Your support means so much, I truly didn't mean to cause any trouble and I am sorry for this uncomfortable situation. I wish we didn't have to tell Ryan; I don't want him worrying about me anymore, but I understand that you both need to be involved with whatever you say to Tracy. It's just so awkward."

"Hey, she made it awkward, not you. I'm going to go back out there. Tracy's shift is almost over so I'll send her home early if you think you can pick up the slack for a bit. Then Ry and I will talk to her tomorrow."

Anna nodded. "Okay, that sounds manageable. Thanks again, Jake."

Jake gave her a brief smile before closing the office door, leaving Anna alone to process what had happened. She still felt bad that her relationship with Ryan had caused an issue at the pub, but was so relieved that Jake didn't seem at all fazed by it.

A few minutes later the door to the office opened once again, and Ryan looked in. When he saw Anna standing by the couch, he came all the way into the office and strode over to her, pulling her into his arms without saying a word. They stood there, locked in each other's arms, for several moments. Slowly, Anna could feel their heartbeats synchronizing, as a peaceful sense of stability and comfort flooded her veins.

Eventually, Ryan pulled away slightly, before looking down at her, an apologetic expression on his handsome face. "Sweetheart, I am so sorry for Tracy. She's fucking nuts if she thinks it's okay to speak to you that way."

"It's fine, honestly. Jake and I talked, and I feel alright about it all. I get that she's just jealous. It did hurt to hear her say the things she said, and I felt weird about it, about us, for a moment, but I'm over it now, I swear."

"Anna, don't you dare feel weird about us. Something that feels so goddamn right can't possibly be wrong. We did nothing wrong. You hear me?"

Anna sighed, letting the strength of Ryan's conviction wash over her. She knew he was right. Their feelings for each other were not wrong, even if the fact that they worked together seemed awkward.

"I hear you. I want to apologize again for making things awkward tonight, but I won't. Because you're right, we—I—did nothing wrong. I won't feel bad about her jealousy."

Ryan's smile was full of warmth and pride and infused her with a confidence she had not felt in a very long time. Slowly, she was learning to stand her ground and not hide behind shame and fear. Emboldened by this new sense of self, Anna pushed Ryan backward until he fell against the small couch. He looked at her with curiosity, smoldering heat growing in his eyes. She straddled his lap, subtly grinding against his cock to tease him. Even if they couldn't take things any further right now, she needed him to feel the depths of her desire and trust in him. Anna knew Ryan would never intentionally put her in a situation that could be negative, but that didn't mean she couldn't tempt him.

She leaned in to press an open-mouthed kiss to the side of his neck. His answering groan confirmed she was on the right track with her seduction. As her lips moved slowly up toward his face, his hands tightened on her hips, as if he had to hold back from taking her right then and there. She reached his mouth and continued to tease, not landing right on his lips but pressing light kisses to the corners, top and bottom. With a growl, Ryan reached his limit of patience and grabbed her head, holding her gently but lovingly in place as he ravaged her mouth. The tables had turned, and Anna knew she was no longer in control; he was, and she happily gave in to his seductive power.

As their tongues danced together, Anna's hands snuck under Ryan's shirt to caress the muscles of his back. When he bit down gently on her lower lip she answered with a light scratch of her nails. She was about to rip off his shirt when a noise outside the office broke through the sexual haze.

"Ohmygod. Ryan, we can't do this here!" Anna gasped, mortified as she realized just how close she had come to getting naked in the office. And she thought the confrontation with Tracy had been awkward.

"Don't worry, the door is locked. But you're right, I can't do everything I want to do with people just outside the door," Ryan said, then looked at her with a wicked gleam in his eyes. "You would make far too much noise."

She slapped away his hands with a laugh as he gently squeezed her breasts. "We'll see who's making too much noise later, big guy. Come on, we had better get back to work."

Anna stood up, pulling him in for one last kiss before taking his hand and confidently walking back out to the bar. She noticed Tracy out of the corner of her eye, but thankfully the other woman didn't say a word. Ryan's hand in hers, and Jake's smile when he saw the two of them, was all the reassurance she needed. And when Ryan squeezed her hand and pressed a kiss to the side of her head in full view of Tracy and the other pub staff, she knew he was by her side, no matter what.

12

Chapter 11

The rest of the evening passed by uneventfully. Tracy went home early without so much as another glance toward either Ryan or Anna. Callie came by for a drink and decided to stay on and chat with Anna as she poured sleeves of beer behind the bar.

Ryan watched the two women laughing together with a strange feeling in his chest. Seeing the two women he cared about, one as a friend—and one as something more— getting along so well, did something inside his heart. Something strange but not unwelcome. He had already been getting glimpses of a future with Anna, but every day it was becoming more and more clear. Seeing Anna and Callie together, he could imagine camping in the summer with Jake and Callie, barbecues with kids running around.

Kids? Now that idea made Ryan quite literally stumble in his tracks. Never in his life had he considered starting a family. Ever. Yet, with Anna fitting so seamlessly into his life and his friendships, he could see that crazy idea becoming a reality.

Jake must have noticed the look of shock on his best friend's face. He gently shoved Ryan by the shoulder before leaning in to speak in a low voice so he wouldn't be overheard. "Dude. What the hell? You look like you're lost in Lalaland."

Ryan startled out of his reverie and became aware of the happy chaos surrounding him at the bar.

"What? Oh. Shit. Sorry, I was just thinking about..." His eyes flickered over to Anna, unable to put words to his feelings.

"Yeah, man, I know what you were thinking about," Jake replied. Then he looked meaningfully over at their two women. One blond, one brunette, both beautiful. "We are fucking lucky. You get that now, right?"

Lucky was one way to describe it. Ryan sighed. "Yeah, I get it."

Although he appreciated how lucky he was to have met Anna, deep inside his mind his old fears battled to be heard. He still didn't trust himself not to screw up somehow and hurt her. Ryan knew that he could only ignore his inner demons for so long before they would begin to consume him. And no words of trust and love from Anna or anyone else could fully eradicate it. No, this was one war he had to wage himself.

* * *

After the pub closed for the evening, Anna sagged into a booth across from Callie. Ryan and Jake were right behind her with a pitcher of beer and four glasses. As she sat there, surrounded by people she knew she could genuinely call friends, Anna marveled at how her life had turned around in such a short time.

Was it really a matter of only a few weeks ago that she was

essentially trapped in Sacramento with Tim, fearful of his mood and always wondering what he would do next? Now, instead of fear and uncertainty, she felt security.

Ryan's arm was slung casually over her shoulders, his fingertips lightly brushing her arm. As he was engrossed in a conversation with Jake, his actions seemed unconscious, or automatic. The idea that it was comfortable and easy for him to show casual affection without needing anything in return was another welcome experience for Anna. She snuggled into his arms, content to be held in his safe embrace.

Across the table, Anna could see Callie looking at the two of them with a satisfied smile on her face. When Callie realized she was looking at her, she slid around the booth to be closer. Leaning in, Callie spoke softly into Anna's ear.

"You're so good for him, Anna. The difference is incredible. Gone is the cocky flirt who just wanted to sleep with every woman that came in here. He's not only serious about you but he's settled into his role as a real partner in the bar as well. It's like he's grown up in a hurry, for the best possible reason."

Anna's heart warmed to hear those words. She hadn't known Ryan as the playboy he apparently used to be, but she absolutely believed that the Ryan she knew, was a mature, kind man who was clearly committed to his friends and to his work.

Wanting to stand up for Ryan, she said, "I don't think I should take that much credit. He's an amazing man, all on his own."

Callie was quick to respond, placing her hand on Anna's shoulder. "Oh, he absolutely is, but trust me when I say you have been a catalyst for him. It's as if he has finally figured out for himself how amazing he can be and is living up to that at last."

With that, Callie slid back over to her side of the booth, before nudging Jake and whispering something in his ear that made his eyes widen and a heated look come into his eyes. They both stood up and said a quick goodbye before they grabbed each other's hands and ran toward the back door, Callie's giggle echoing back into the empty bar.

Ryan turned to Anna with a grin. "Well, it doesn't take an idiot to guess what they're rushing off to do. Are you ready to go home?" He slid out of the booth and reached a hand down to help her.

She let him pull her up, before wrapping her arms around his stomach. She looked up at him with an answering smile. "Yeah I'm ready. But you know, Sally asked to have Samson over tonight because she misses him, so I'm not in a rush to get to my house..."

The heat that came into Ryan's beautiful blue eyes was such a confidence boost for Anna. His obvious sexual attraction to her was so empowering.

"I'm not going to lie, sweetheart, I'm dying to be inside you again. I really want to see you spread out on my bed. Can we go back to my place tonight?"

The heat that was always smoldering between the two of them, like the coals in a banked fire, sparked into flames that sent a wave of heat straight through her. Feeling bold, she slid her hand down his torso to cup his already firm cock through his jeans. Marveling at the fact that she could feel him hardening just from her touch, Anna simply nodded at Ryan, before using her other hand to pull his head down to meet hers in a passionate kiss.

Ryan quickly took command of the kiss. His mouth captured hers in its protective embrace. Passion radiated between them as their tongues tangled, awakening a deep desire within her, unlike anything she had ever felt before. She had never been with a man who could be equal parts gentle and powerful, romantic, and erotic, all in one kiss. As his hand slid confidently up her neck to tangle in her hair, she moaned at the sensation of the slight tug on her scalp. She felt a soul-deep surrender to his blissful protection and in that instant, she knew that Ryan would guard her heart and her body from anything.

* * *

Ryan honestly didn't know if he would ever get enough of Anna's kisses. They were a drug he never expected to become addicted to, yet here he was chasing another high.

Breaking apart finally, he was pleased to see the flush on her cheeks, and noticed she was breathing just as heavily as he was. This woman affected him in a way no one ever had before, and he damn well loved it.

"I need to get you home. Now, before we do things in this bar that Jake would murder me for." Ryan paused for a moment. "Come to think of it, who the fuck knows if he and Callie have already screwed around in here."

Anna's tinkling laugh was becoming his favorite sound ever. If he could hear nothing but that for the rest of his life, that would be a pretty damn fine life.

"Well, I'd rather not make it even more awkward to work here, thank you very much. It's hard enough wanting to kiss my boss every time I see him."

Anna's coy smile drove him crazy. So crazy he had to make her laugh again. "Wait. You want to kiss Jake? What the hell!"

The giggle and eye roll she gave him in response was perfection. Seeing Anna as a relaxed and happy woman made Ryan feel ten feet tall for his part in helping her let go of her fear.

"Alright, you goof, let's go. Take me home and then... take me." Anna winked saucily as she pulled him down the hallway toward the back door. All he could do was laugh and follow the woman of his dreams.

* * *

The drive to Ryan's house was blessedly short. Anna was surprised by how the teasing banter at the bar had been a major turn on for her. There was something about the way Ryan made her feel at ease that was far more attractive than any grand gesture.

Ryan pulled the truck into a parking spot in front of a low apartment building. In the dark she couldn't make out much, but it seemed to be well maintained. He hopped out and quickly jogged around to her side of the truck to open the door and help her down—not that she needed it, but his chivalry was touching.

He led her in through the front door and quickly to the elevator. When the doors closed behind them, he spun her around and pushed her against the wall. Possessed by passion, their hands grabbed at each other, reaching beneath their shirts, desperate to find bare skin to touch. Anna moaned as Ryan alternated between nibbling and gently sucking at the skin on the side of her neck and along her collarbone. Her hands dug into his firm abs, before snaking around to grab his ass and pull him even closer to her.

"Oh god, Ryan." She gasped as his lips continued to torment.

She was burning up inside, desperate to reach the privacy of his apartment. When the elevator finally came to a stop, Ryan swept her up into his arms and strode purposefully toward his door. Proving his strength by keeping her in his arms, he somehow managed to unlock the door. Once inside the dark apartment, the overwhelming sexual tension magically eased. The urgency was gone, replaced by a mutual need to slow down and savor the connection building between them.

He continued to kiss her as he slowly peeled off her jacket. In between pressing his lips to her skin, he spoke in a voice that was agonizingly low and seductive. "I'm going to get you naked, and feast on your body, worshiping you."

She was incredibly aroused by the heat behind his words, but Anna was aware that after a full shift at the bar, she was not exactly fresh. The idea of showering together, hot water cascading down Ryan's muscled body, was so erotic, she knew she had to make that vision a reality. She leaned back just far enough that he had to stop kissing her, which made him raise his eyes questioningly.

"Trust me I want that too, but we both smell like beer and sweat. How about a shower first?"

Ryan grinned wickedly at her, a twinkle in his eyes. "I like it. Get down and dirty while getting clean."

With that he smacked her lightly on her ass before leading her down a short hallway to a small yet tidy bathroom. She watched him open the door to the shower and turn the tap on. As the water began to warm up, his eyes turned back to her with an intense look of passion. He slowly lifted her shirt over her head, before leaning down to press a soft kiss between her breasts. When he then lifted his own shirt over his head, Anna let her fingers trail up and down his torso, watching his nipples pebble in response when her nails lightly scraped over them.

Back and forth they slowly undressed each other as steam billowed out of the shower, enveloping them in a dense heat that mirrored the heat building inside their bodies.

Anna stepped into the shower first, and let the water fall down her back. When she turned to look at Ryan she was stunned by the wild look in his eyes. In one swift move he was in the shower with her, lifting her easily into his arms again. He devoured her lips in a kiss as he pressed her back against the shower wall, and with the steaming hot water cascading down between their bodies, he began a slow grind against her that had Anna moaning into his mouth.

Eager to give as much pleasure as she had already received, she pushed him away, and dropped to her knees. Without a word she began to gently stroke his rock-hard cock, examining it in wonder. The hair at the base was neatly trimmed, making it stand proudly out from his body. Anna was overcome with a desire to taste him, so when her strokes brought a drop of fluid out of the tip, she leaned in and licked it up.

"Fuck. The anticipation of your mouth on me is the best kind of torture," Ryan growled, sending shivers down Anna's spine, despite the heat from the shower pounding down onto her. In response she opened her mouth and took him in as far as she could. Gradually she worked into a rhythm with her hands and her mouth. She felt powerful, even on her knees, knowing she could bring this sexy, confident man such pleasure.

She could tell he was getting close as his cock grew even larger in her mouth. Ryan hesitated, and looked down at her, frozen. "You don't have to, Anna..."

Anna winked at him and sped up her movements, causing a groan to fall out of Ryan's mouth. Seconds later he orgasmed sending hot jets of musky fluid into her mouth. She swallowed every drop, pleased to look up and see Ryan breathing heavily with his eyes closed, overcome by his release.

Standing up slowly, Anna took the bar of soap and began to rub it over Ryan's body. She was content to take care of him this way, knowing he would certainly be taking care of her soon. Sure enough, he opened his eyes at her gentle touch and covered her hands with his own. Without a word he took the soap and began massaging her body, starting at her shoulders, and working his way down. He stared into her eyes as he caressed her breasts, teasing her nipples until they were stiff with desire. She gasped when he gently pinched one, then moaned when he rinsed the soap away, then swiftly leaned down and kissed where he had pinched. Slowly, silently, he moved over her body washing her, letting the warm water rinse away the soap, and then following with his lips. As he had promised, he worshiped her.

When Ryan had made his way down her legs, he tortured her by avoiding the one place she wanted him the most. Suddenly he stood up and turned off the water. The silence between them was charged with erotic sensuality. Anna loved watching his face and seeing the intensity there.

He continued his ministrations by wrapping her in a fluffy towel and gently drying her before quickly rubbing his own body dry. Then he led her out of the bathroom and into what was obviously his bedroom. Anna looked around, curious to see his private space. She was surprised by how tidy it was, with a pile of clothes folded on a chair in the corner and a large king-sized bed neatly made with dark blue sheets. This was where Ryan stopped, with Anna standing so her legs were against the bed. Finally, he spoke. "There are no words for me to describe the way you make me feel, Anna. So, I'm going to show you."

He gently pushed her down to sit on the bed, then knelt in between her legs. Spreading them apart, he reverently ran his hands up the inside of her thighs. With a sigh, Anna lay back on the soft duvet. She closed her eyes and gave in to the sensation of Ryan's hands and lips slowly making their way closer and closer to her center where heat and moisture were beginning to pool. When he kissed her just above her clit, she moaned, desperate for relief from the pressure that was building inside.

"Damn, you smell so fucking fantastic, sweetheart."

Anna never knew dirty talk could turn her on so powerfully, but she squirmed at his words. Thankfully he didn't make her wait any longer, and the next thing she felt was his warm tongue firmly stroking her sex. His magical fingers and tongue whipped her into a frenzy within minutes. He drove his fingers in and out, curling them over to tease her G-spot, as his tongue laved her clit. The sensations were so intense that one of his arms had to hold her down by the hips as she thrashed on the bed, consumed with pleasure. She grabbed his hair, holding him in place as she moaned and whimpered in response to his seduction.

It didn't take long for Anna to feel her release coming closer and closer, and as she felt her body clench around Ryan's finger in anticipation, she could no longer hold back her cries of passion.

"Ryan, ohgodohgodohgod, Ryan, YES!"

She couldn't hold back a scream as she cascaded into a powerful orgasm, drawn out by Ryan's continued licks and sucks at her clit. When at last her body stopped shuddering with the after-effects, he had moved up beside her and pulled her into his arms. She nestled in, grateful for the time to come down from that spectacular release.

After a few moments, she could feel his solid cock pressing into her side. She sat up and straddled his body, bringing his rigid length into direct contact with her still-throbbing sex.

"You are the most stunning woman in the world when you climax." Ryan spoke softly but with passion as he brushed some hair behind her ear. His blue eyes were shimmering with something Anna wanted to say could be love, but she was scared to ask. Instead she chose to respond to his beautiful words with words of her own.

"Then why don't you make me do it again."

She reached down, grabbed his cock, and fit it to the entrance of her channel. Shifting forward, the first couple of inches of his cock slid inside her wet heat. As they let out a simultaneous sound of arousal, realization hit them that Ryan didn't have on a condom.

"Holy fuck, sweetheart that feels amazing. But I really should..."

Anna was suddenly gripped by the awareness that she had never thought to get tested after leaving Tim. Even though they were not intimate often, she knew he was not faithful. She froze, hovering on her knees over Ryan's cock, before climbing off him and sinking down onto the bed beside him.

"Oh my god. I'm such a fool. After Tim, I didn't think I would... I mean I haven't... I don't know..." She was so embarrassed, and so flustered by what she was trying to say. Thankfully, Ryan seemed to know what she was getting at. He grabbed her face, forcing her to look at him.

"Anna, don't worry. Nothing happened, and I'm not that worried. We'll use condoms, and if it'll make you feel better, I'm sure Callie can help you get tested. I'm clean by the way," he said with a wink and a warm smile. "But no matter what a test says, I'm not going to be able to keep away from you, so don't get any ideas."

Anna laughed, grateful for how quickly he had put her mind at ease. Her laugh turned into a gasp as Ryan swung her legs back over his, so she was once again straddling him. He rubbed his hands up and down her thighs.

"You're in control." Ryan's voice was quiet, but serious.

Anna realized he was waiting for her to decide what would happen next. She loved the fact that his actions supported his words, proving he meant them. She reached over to the side table, making sure to lean low enough that her breasts grazed Ryan's body eliciting a low groan and a tightening of his fingers, and grabbed a condom. Then she shifted backward so that she could roll it down his rigid length, never letting her eyes leave his. She knew that the sensual burn she could feel inside was mirrored in his eyes.

With protection on, Anna once again used her hands to slowly guide his cock into her slippery channel. When he was seated deeply inside of her, she began to rock her hips back and forth, reveling in the feel of him hitting her inner walls and the friction as she moved.

"I love the way you fill me up," she gasped.

"You're so fucking tight around me," he replied with a growl, causing Anna to shiver in response.

As she played with her breasts, undulating her body over top of his, she lost herself in the passion of the moment. Unable to feel where she ended and he began, their bodies moved together toward the ultimate release.

Ryan took over and thrust his hips even higher, going deeper than Anna had thought possible. With each thrust he angled himself to rub along her clit, doubling the arousal. She was vaguely aware that she was sighing his name over and over with every movement. As she edged closer and closer to her climax, she lost all sense of time and place, consumed by the overpowering physical and emotional connection being forged between them.

When he let out a guttural groan, she felt him swell inside of her, and knew he was seconds away from orgasm. As soon as his strong fingers touched her clit, she shot over the edge with him. Their shouts of release mingled together as she collapsed down onto his chest, utterly spent by what had just happened.

After breathing heavily for several minutes, Anna felt both of their heart rates return to normal. Lifting her head, she smiled hesitantly at Ryan. "The way you touch me, make love to me, it's just so..." She was at a loss for words. How could she describe the depth of feelings she was developing, without scaring him off? Thankfully, his response was exactly what she needed to hear.

"I know, Anna. It's just so... for me too."

Ryan's answering smile was full of warmth and emotion waiting to be shared. But she could tell he too was holding back. Maybe it was just too soon for them both.

He shifted underneath her, and Anna slid over. Ryan pressed a kiss to her shoulder before walking unabashedly naked into the bathroom to dispose of the condom. When he came back, he climbed back into bed and pulled Anna into his side with a contented sigh. She looked up to see his eyes closed, and a very satisfied smile on his face.

As if he could feel her gaze, Ryan opened his eyes and looked down at her, squeezing her even tighter into his side. "You are such a different person from the woman who walked into my bar in January. Now, you're so strong, and confident, and sexy as hell. You amaze me."

Anna was speechless. He really saw her as strong and confident?

"Wow. I... I wish I felt that way. I want to feel brave and strong, but honestly the only time I feel safe is with you." When she felt Ryan shift, she quickly went on, "That isn't exactly a bad thing, I love how you want to take care of me. I just also want to be strong on my own. I don't want to live my life scared of my past, you know?"

Ryan was quiet for a moment. Anna lay still, waiting to hear his reply. His hand was lightly stroking up and down her back, comforting her, reassuring her of his solid presence.

"Sweetheart, I want nothing more than for you to see yourself the way I do. I'm in support of whatever we need to do, to help you feel like the incredible woman you are. Have you thought of self-defense classes? It might help you feel more confident about your own strength."

Anna sat up quickly, the sheet pooling around her waist. She stared down at Ryan with a smile growing on her face.

"Oh, that's a perfect idea!"

He sat up beside her. "I bet Callie would join you, maybe even her friends Reagan and Melanie. It might be nice for you to meet some more amazing women," he added gently.

"Okay. I'll call Callie tomorrow," she replied.

"Great. Now get back here." Ryan gently tugged her back into his arms, and she snuggled in tightly. His solid chest was a surprisingly comfortable pillow, and she felt the exhaustion of both a long shift and multiple orgasms overcome her.

She soon fell asleep, tangled in his arms, a peaceful smile on her face. Content that she was working toward a life that would finally be her own.

13

Chapter 12

In less than a week, Anna and Callie found a self-defense class at a local gym and had asked Callie's friends Reagan and Melanie to join them. The women decided to meet before the class at the juice bar next to the gym. As they sat there chatting, Anna looked at the group with mixed feelings. It was amazing to build new friendships, especially with such incredible women, but she was still nervous. Would they want to know why she had suggested the class? She wasn't ready to tell them all of her story; she didn't know if she could handle their looks of pity or judgement.

When they walked into the gym where the class would be held, Reagan whispered under her breath so that only the four of them could hear, "Damnit, look at us. A room full of beautiful, strong women, and we are all here because we need to learn how to protect ourselves from assholes masquerading as men. What the hell is wrong with this world?"

The other women murmured their agreement as they went to find their places. The instructors arrived, a small, dark-haired woman with an innocent, child-like appearance and, standing just behind her, was a strong bald man who certainly wasn't someone Anna would want to meet in a dark alley.

Anna gave a gasp of surprise, echoed by everyone else in the class, when the session began not with introductions, but with a demonstration. Before they could register what was happening, the large, bald man went to grab the female instructor from behind. In one seamless maneuver, she twisted her body just enough to drive an elbow into his gut and her fist up toward his nose, before she sprinted to the other side of the gym.

From the far side of the room, the female instructor called out to the class, "Still think we're the weaker sex? You won't by the time I'm done with you!" To which the class erupted in cheers.

* * *

Two hours later, Anna and her friends spilled out of the gym, sweaty and exhilarated with how strong and empowered they all felt.

"That was freaking BADASS!" Melanie shouted with a pump of her arm in the air. One of Callie's fellow ER physicians, she was an outspoken, energetic woman.

"I know, right? I had no idea there were so many ways to drop a guy to the floor," Reagan added enthusiastically.

"Why do women have to be the ones to learn new behavior? Why the hell can't guys just stop being abusive assholes?" Anna blurted out the words without thinking.

Callie swung her arm over Anna's shoulders. "You're right, it would be so much easier if men just respected women. But, until that magical day, I think it's great that more women are learning how to protect themselves. So, I personally want to thank you for inviting us to the class with you. Even with Jake in my life, who I know wouldn't dream of ever hurting me, I feel better knowing that if he wasn't around I could still defend myself."

Melanie and Reagan both nodded their agreement.

"Yeah, Anna, you and Callie found two great guys, which is so amazing. But for those of us still in the dating game," Reagan shuddered, "it's a nightmare. Now at least I know I could fend someone off if I had to. Although I hope like hell I never do."

Melanie sighed. "I'm not even remotely interested in another relationship, so as a happily divorced and proudly single lady, I have to agree with Reagan. It can be really freaking scary out there. I can't go anywhere without worrying about some asshole trying to take advantage of me." She quickly looked to Callie apologetically. "Even The Lucky Strike has its share of douchebags, and we all know Jake and Ryan try their best to keep them out."

Callie placed an understanding hand on Melanie's shoulder. "You're right, they try. I think we all wish they didn't have to." She clapped her hands together, clearly trying to shift the mood. "Speaking of The Lucky Strike, who wants to go and see if we can score some free drinks? Anna and I might just have an 'in' with the owners." With a laugh, the women headed to their cars, chatting among themselves about the class.

On her way home, Anna thought about this new, amazing facet to her life in Portland. When she was trapped in Sacramento, she had felt so alone and that no one could possibly understand how she had ended up in the situation she was in. Yet here she was, surrounded by women who would likely not only believe her, but would probably support her just as they supported each other. This was the type of friendship she hadn't even realized she was longing for.

And once again, it was all thanks to Ryan.

* * *

Back at her house, Anna showered and changed out of her workout clothes, still lost in thought about the many changes in her life over the last several weeks. By chance she had stumbled into the pub that snowy night, desperate to escape Tim's clutches. Doing so, she had found more than she ever expected, a job, friends, and Ryan. The impossibly sexy man who had turned her world upside down in the best possible way. She knew her feelings for him were growing beyond anything she had ever hoped to find. He did more than make her feel safe, he made her feel strong, cherished, and capable. He picked her up out of the darkest time of her life and lifted her into the light, helping her to stand on her own two feet again.

She grinned to herself, eager to see him, touch him, try to show him just how much he was coming to mean to her. She knew she was not yet ready to say those three little words, but if Anna was being honest with herself... that was definitely where she seemed to be headed.

A knock at her front door snapped her back to the present. She knew it had to be Callie, picking her up to go to the bar. With a final swipe of lip gloss and a pat on the head for Samson, she grabbed her jacket and headed out the door.

"Someone looks excited... I wonder why!" Callie teased as she followed Anna down the path to her car.

Anna looked over her shoulder at her friend. "You know

exactly why, and don't think your smile is any less excited! Let's go and see those men of ours."

Callie laughed. "Okay, okay, let's go."

Settling into her seat, Anna could feel the smile stretching across her face. Maybe it was still the endorphin high from the self-defense class, but she felt on top of the world. As if she could do anything. Everything was looking up, and she felt happier than she had in a long time.

But lurking behind that happiness were the sinister fears that never left. If Tim ever realized that she not only witnessed what he did, but had video proof of it, he wouldn't rest until he found Anna. The only question was, what would he do when he finally caught up to her?

14

Chapter 13

"Dude, if you look at the door with those puppy dog eyes one more time, I'm going to punch you," Ryan's brother, Noah, teased him from his seat across the bar.

Ryan could feel the telltale heat of embarrassment flood his face as he blushed, not wanting to admit that he had been anxiously watching for Anna to appear for the last hour. He knew the ladies were planning to stop by because of a text message Callie had sent Jake. When Noah came in to the pub for a drink, Ryan had eagerly told him that Anna was coming. It was so out of character for Ryan to be excited about introducing a woman to his family, that Noah hadn't stopped giving him a hard time.

"Fuck off, man. You're just jealous."

"Nah, I'm just waiting for another drink and you're so distracted you haven't even realized it yet."

Ryan rolled his eyes as he grabbed his brother's glass and started to pour him another beer. So what if he was distracted. Anna was the best kind of distraction. Beautiful, smart, kind, sexy, and those little noises she made when she...

"RYAN! Shit, man, you just got beer everywhere."

Ryan snapped back to reality and realized he had overfilled the glass, and the lager Noah wanted was swamping the bar top and dripping onto the floor.

"Damnit." He grabbed a towel and started to mop it up, not looking Noah in the eye, knowing that his brother would tease him mercilessly.

"Hey, handsome." Anna's soft voice pierced through his distracted, embarrassed fog. He looked up, to be met by her sparkling eyes smiling at him. Grinning in response, not caring if his brother or anyone else saw, Ryan reached over the bar, grabbed the back of Anna's head and pulled her close, desperate to feel her lips on his. As their breath mingled together, he felt a shifting in his universe, as if the world were righting itself around him.

"Hey yourself. How was the class?" Ryan held onto her hand across the top of the wooden bar.

Anna peeked curiously at Noah who was smiling as he openly watched the two of them.

"It was amazing." She turned to Noah. "Ummm hi, are you Ryan's brother?"

Noah grinned in response. "I sure am. His more handsome, older brother. I'm Noah, and I can't tell you how amazing it is to meet you. I never thought I'd see the day this jackass would find a woman who made him act like a fool." Then he pulled Anna into his arms for a hug, eliciting a growl from Ryan who still stood behind the bar.

"Oh fuck off, Noah." Ryan groaned. He knew his brother wouldn't hold back in trying to embarrass him in front of Anna.

Thankfully, she just laughed, her adorable giggle making his heart—and another body part—swell with desire.

"Nice to meet you, Noah. Ignore Ryan, I want to hear all the funny stories you've got about him."

Noah stood, and offered his arm to Anna with a ridiculous bow. "Well then, my lady, let us retire away from the help, and I shall regale you with tales of old."

He knew Noah was no threat to him, but Ryan still didn't like the idea of not having Anna nearby. He watched helplessly, as Anna blew him a kiss before wandering off to an open booth with Noah. When she threw her head back and laughed at something Noah said, Ryan's lips pressed into a thin line of jealousy. He wanted to be the one making her laugh like that, and not be stuck behind the bar.

With impeccable timing, Jake and Callie came walking out from the back hallway, hand in hand. Ryan took in Callie's messed-up hair and Jake's satisfied grin and knew his best friend had been luckier than he had in spending time with his girl. Suddenly Ryan knew how he could get a break from bartending.

"Hey, lovebirds. Think you can tear yourselves away from each other long enough to help me? While you were getting busy, my brother was moving in on my girl."

Jake glanced over at the booth where Noah and Anna were talking animatedly, then looked back at Ryan with a knowing look. "Feeling worried she might want the older Carlisle?" he teased.

Callie smacked his arm lightly, before turning to Ryan. "Oh relax, you've got nothing to worry about, Ryan. That woman is crazy for you." She looked up at Jake. "Come on, hot bartender, pour me a beer."

Ryan shot Callie a grateful look as he rounded the end of the bar, with a sleeve of Anna's favorite beer in his hand. He strode over to the booth and slid in next to her, placed the beer in front of her and tugged her into his side protectively before glaring at his brother.

"Whatever he's told you, it's all lies."

Her answering laugh and the feel of her hand on his leg soothed him, and Ryan relaxed into the cushioned bench seat, letting the chatter between Noah and Anna wash over him. He hadn't really been that worried about what Noah would say. His brother was such a romantic, Ryan knew that Noah would want him to be happy no matter what.

A while later, the bar had filled with people waiting for Chase to come on stage and sing. Ryan glanced at the bar and saw Jake was slammed with customers.

"Sorry, sweetheart, I have to get back to work," he said regretfully as he slid out of the booth.

Noah followed him out. "Yeah, I actually need to head home as well. It was nice to meet you Anna, hopefully we'll see you again soon." He gave Anna a swift hug, clapped Ryan on his back and headed for the door.

Ryan bent down and kissed Anna firmly on the mouth. "It was nice seeing you and my brother getting along so well."

"He's very easy to get along with," Anna replied. "You're both such handsome, friendly men."

"Just remember which brother you're with," Ryan growled, holding her tightly and pressing their bodies together.

Anna reached her hands around his back and tucked them into his back pockets so she could gently squeeze his ass. "Oh, I know which Carlisle brother I'm with. It's the one who is sexy as sin and can turn me on with nothing more than his growly voice."

Letting out a groan as her sultry words made his cock twitch,

Ryan touched his forehead to hers. Taking a deep breath, he tried to get his reaction to her under control. "You have no idea how much you drive me crazy. It's the best feeling in the world."

* * *

Anna watched Ryan go back to work, as Reagan and Callie walked over with a pitcher of beer and three glasses. Melanie had sent them a message saying she couldn't join them for drinks after all, so it would just be the three of them.

"I mean it, Reagan, you have to stop sending all of those brownies home with Jake and I. Just hurry up and open your bakery, preferably before I end up in a brownie coma." Callie's teasing reached Anna's ears, and she looked at the women with curiosity.

"A bakery? Is that your plan Reagan?" Anna was interested to hear the response. From what little she knew about her, she thought Reagan worked in an office somewhere downtown.

Reagan snorted and rolled her eyes. "That's Callie's plan, and my foolish dream."

Callie looked at her with compassion. "It's not foolish. It's your passion, and you're crazy if you don't pursue it."

Reagan was silent, looking down at the table, tearing a napkin into tiny pieces. Anna instinctively knew Reagan was feeling self-conscious about herself and her dreams.

"Did you know I was in college studying to be a teacher?" If opening up about her past could help Reagan overcome her fears, then maybe it was time for Anna to share a little bit more. "I moved to California for school. If things had turned out differently, I would've been a kindergarten teacher by now." Anna sighed, remembering how excited she and Aunt Theresa had been. The plan was for Anna to get her degree in California, and then return to Portland to teach.

"Instead I ended up in a terrible relationship." Anna hesitated, then took the plunge. "He stole my dream from me. The guy I was with. He took over my life, and robbed me of my friends, my family, my happiness, and my future. It was awful, in so many ways. But what matters right now is this: No one should have to give up their dreams. Not because of some asshole trying to control them, and certainly not because they're too scared to try."

Reagan looked at her, not with pity, but with compassion and admiration. She reached over to touch Anna's hand. "I'm so sorry, Anna. You are one hell of a strong woman to have made it out of a relationship like that. I know you're right, I'm the only person holding myself back. Which is so stupid."

"It's not stupid, Reags. It's hard to imagine taking such a huge leap of faith," Callie held Reagan's gaze with loving determination, "but I know how unhappy you are working a crappy job, with a jerk of a boss. And, you are an incredible baker. I honestly think your brownies could be a major success."

"A fear of failure is understandable. But what do you fear most? Failing, or never trying," Anna chimed in.

Reagan sagged back into her seat. "I know, I know. Be brave, reach for the stars, all that bull." She straightened up and looked pointedly at Anna. "I'll make you a deal. I will give some serious consideration to opening a bakery, if you'll think about going back to school. Reclaim your dreams, Anna, and don't let the asshole win."

Anna gave Reagan a small smile and nodded. "Okay, I'll look

into it. We can be brave together."

Callie lifted her glass in response. "Cheers to that ladies. We are three badass women, achieving our dreams and living our best lives."

As the girls laughed and clinked their glasses together, Anna found herself filled with a nervous excitement at the thought of going back to school. Maybe reclaiming her dream of being a kindergarten teacher was the perfect way for her to feel like she had her life back after Tim destroyed it all.

Fast on the heels of that excitement came dread. How could she possibly plan for a future, when there was a very real chance that Tim would find her? She shivered, as fear laced through her at the thought of what he might do to her when he found her.

Oblivious to the undercurrent of Anna's emotions. Callie and Reagan had carried on laughing and talking. Jake's voice suddenly boomed over the speakers, announcing that Chase would be performing in five minutes.

"Oooh, Reagan, your man is coming on soon!" Callie nudged Reagan playfully.

"Are you dating Chase?" Anna asked, surprised that Ryan had not mentioned that the two were together.

"Oh my god, no! Callie is just being annoying." Reagan's face went bright red under her auburn hair.

"But she wants to," Callie exclaimed brightly. "I still don't know how you are so oblivious to the fact that he basically stares at you the entire time he's on stage. He's got it bad."

Reagan scoffed. "You're delusional, Cal. Now can we just drink and enjoy the music please?"

"Uh huh, the music. Sure. That's what we'll be enjoying..."

Anna giggled at the easy teasing between Callie and Reagan.

She thought wistfully how nice it must be to have that kind of easy and close friendship. That was one thing she'd never had, even before Tim. With her parents passing, and then moving in with Aunt Theresa, she hadn't had the chance to form deep friendships. Maybe someday, she could settle down long enough for that to be possible.

Callie turned her attention back to Anna. "Anna, tell Reagan she's insane for thinking Chase isn't interested in her. Just watch the way he looks at her when he sings. I swear the heat that he projects could burn this place down!"

As the handsome singer took to the stage, Anna watched him closely. Sure enough, his gaze strayed to Reagan frequently as he sang a cover of Maroon 5's song 'It Was Always You.'

Callie leaned over to speak softly so only Reagan and Anna could hear. "You hear those words? He's singing that to you, Reags."

Reagan blushed, but didn't say a word. Anna noticed how her eyes were trained solely on Chase, electricity jumping between the two of them. She had to agree with Callie. Reagan had to be blind not to see the attraction he held for her. Hopefully, it would only be a matter of time before one of them was brave enough to do something about it.

* * *

Ryan watched Chase on stage from behind the bar. His energy and talent certainly brought in a crowd every time he performed at the pub.

"Signing him was the best business decision we've made." Jake's words confirmed Ryan's opinion.

"Damn right. Hey after this set, let's hand the bar over to Mark and sit down with the girls for a bit," Ryan replied.

Jake ran his hands through his hair, a telltale sign that he was stressed. "That sounds perfect, I need a drink."

"Everything okay?"

"Oh yeah, everything's awesome. Just busy. Trying to plan a wedding, run a business, and somehow have time for my fiancée is not easy."

Ryan could feel empathy for his friend, but had to get a dig in. "You're just getting too old, bro. I guess Callie's too much for you to handle already."

"Shut up. You're only younger than me by a few months. Callie is not too much. She's fucking perfect. I just want to give her everything, but I can't do that and be here so much." Jake sighed, "I'm sorry. I don't mean to dump all over you, Ry. It's fine, really. We're doing so well with the pub; I should be happy."

"Well sure, we can be happy about our success, but that doesn't mean we have to keep going at this pace. Like you said, we are doing well, so maybe we need to hire a manager or something. Somebody who can take on some of the administrative stuff for you, and maybe take over some of the bartending shifts for me too." Ryan was quiet for a moment, envisioning his future. "Who knows, maybe someday I'll be where you are, trying to plan a wedding and think about a family. We can't be giving everything to this place forever."

"Wait a fucking minute. Is Ryan 'the playboy' Carlisle talking about settling down someday?" Jake's voice was incredulous as he carefully studied his best friend to see if he was serious.

"Yeah, man, I guess I am. It's Anna. She makes me want things I never thought I would want. It's fucking terrifying, but, kind of cool too." Ryan shrugged, not afraid to admit to Jake how serious he was feeling. "I can see a future with her. She's incredible."

"Damn. I'm happy for you, man, let's go and have a drink with our incredible women," Jake replied as he slung his arm over Ryan's shoulders, and the two men walked over to the booth. Ryan could feel his pulse jump just looking at Anna. She was beyond incredible. She was the only thing that soothed an ache inside him, an ache he had not known existed until she came into his life and cracked the shell surrounding his heart. An ache for a love that he could call his own.

Sitting down beside Anna, he pulled her in to press a kiss to the side of her head. It felt intimate, despite being such a simple action. As if he was marking her as his.

15

Chapter 14

Soon after finishing his last song, Chase joined the group of friends. Anna looked around and felt warmth suffusing her as she realized she was surrounded by people who genuinely cared for each other, and for her. She smiled to herself as she noticed Chase stare longingly at Reagan, who seemed determined to avoid his gaze. The chemistry between those two was palpable, even to someone like Anna who didn't really know either of them very well.

She was pulled back into the conversation when she heard Callie mentioning the self-defense class. Anna froze momentarily, waiting to see what Callie would say about why they had gone in the first place. She couldn't be open about her past, not when she still held onto a very real fear that someday, everything would be stolen from her when Tim found her.

She felt her shoulders relax when she heard Callie speak.

"We all just wanted to feel strong and capable of taking care of ourselves. I mean, sure, we have you guys, and you're amazing and respect us, and know how to treat women well. But you're not always around, and many men are not as amazing as you three, and Noah even though he's not here right now." Callie smiled at the men sitting with them, and Anna realized Callie was right. She was surrounded by not just wonderful, strong women, but respectful and powerful men.

Ryan raised his glass to toast Callie's words. "We're the lucky ones, to have such incredible women in our lives." A wicked smile came over his face. "Cheers to the assholes who were not good enough for you. I personally want to thank them for leading each of you here, to us, and by thank them, I mean with a punch to the face."

The table erupted with laughter and responding cheers as everyone drank to those words. Ryan leaned over to whisper softly in Anna's ear, "Words can't begin to describe my rage over what happened to you. But I would be lying if I didn't admit that I am so grateful you ended up in my bar, and in my arms."

Anna turned to him, and lifted her hand to brush against his cheek. "I'm grateful too. I never wanted to be trapped with someone like Tim for so long, so I refuse to give him any credit for us meeting. Instead, I'm grateful to Aunt Theresa for loving me, and giving me her house. That's what really brought me to Portland, and to you," she replied, her voice infused with gratitude and affection.

Ryan lifted his glass again, in a private toast between the two of them. His voice was solemn, and laden with emotion.

"To Aunt Theresa."

Tears were building behind Anna's eyes, and she blinked to try and keep them away. Giving Ryan a small smile, she drank to his toast. *Thank you, Aunt Theresa, thank you for saving my life.* As the words crossed her mind, she realized just how true they were. Deep down she knew, if she had stayed with Tim after learning the truth about him, her life would never have been safe. Even here, hundreds of miles away from him, the threat still loomed. But tonight, in Ryan's arms, with friends around her, Anna chose to feel safe. To feel happy.

* * *

Ryan was more content, and happier with his life than ever before. He suspected that nothing could top this, not even playing soccer in the pro-league would have come close to how fulfilled he felt right now. Looking around the bar, now empty of customers, he took in the sight and sound of his friends laughing as they all put on their coats ready to head home. When his eyes landed on Anna, just in time to see her laughing at something Callie was saying, he could swear he felt his heart skip a beat. She was quickly becoming the center of everything in his life, and instead of running scared, all Ryan wanted to do was run toward her, toward their future.

Striding over to her, Ryan wrapped his arms around her, pulling her back against him. He leaned down, loving how petite she felt in his arms. "Let me take you home, sweetheart. Tonight has been so amazing, I don't want it to end."

She twisted in his arms to give him a sultry smile. "I don't either. You'll stay with me tonight?"

"That's not even a question." He captured her upturned lips in a passionate kiss. Vaguely aware of the others leaving, Ryan deepened their embrace, pressing her even tighter into his body. He wanted to lose himself in her, forget where he ended and Anna began. Their tongues danced together, and the little moans Anna was making caused an answering growl to come from his throat. He pressed his hard length against her, reaching his hands down to cup her ass. When she gasped, Ryan let go of even more control and swept her up into his arms. Ignoring the cheers and laughs of their friends who were watching, Ryan carried Anna toward the back door. He effortlessly walked to his truck, reveling in the feel of the feather-light kisses Anna was pressing to his neck.

"Anna, baby, you've got me so turned on I don't know how I'll wait to get you home to take you."

The sexual tension in his voice was palpable and earned a breathy sigh from Anna as she slowly unwound herself from his embrace and climbed into the passenger seat. Ryan quickly got in as well and pulled her across the bench seat to tuck her securely into his side.

"Won't I be distracting if I sit this close?" Anna was the best kind of sultry tease as she pressed even closer to his body.

"You'll be more of a distraction if you're too far away for me to touch, sweetheart."

With a final glance and searing kiss, Ryan put both of his hands firmly on the steering wheel and forced his mind to focus on driving them safely back to Anna's house. He felt Anna relax into his side with a soft sound of contentment.

The drive home was silent, but it didn't take words to convey the heat and emotion sparking between them. Anticipation, mixed with their own unique, romantic chemistry filled the cab of the truck with a pheromone laden energy that hummed with sensual desire.

Feeling deeply thankful that Anna's house was a short drive from the bar, Ryan pulled into her driveway and let out a breath he had not realized he'd been holding. As that last vestige of control started to slip away, he leaned back against his headrest, closing his eyes, and welcoming the wave of desire he had been keeping at bay.

"Well, that was torture. Forgive me for going caveman, but if you do not get your sweet ass inside that house and naked in the next few seconds, I can't be held responsible for what I might do." He turned a searing look on her, scorching the air between them. In the back of his mind was a twinge of discomfort, wondering if his words were too aggressive. But the answering gasp of passion from Anna, combined with her scrambling to get out of the truck and run to the house brought a wolfish grin to his face. Locking the truck behind him, he ran up behind her before sweeping her up in his arms, earning a squeal of laughter from her.

"Why are you so obsessed with carrying me! How am I meant to open the door and get naked when I'm stuck in your arms, big guy?" Anna teased, passion lighting her face.

"I'm sure we can find a way." Ryan shifted her in his arms, taking the key from her and unlocking the front door. "I've decided you need to be in my arms all the time."

"If you insist." She laughed, before pressing a lighthearted kiss to his nose.

As the door swung open, Samson's welcoming bark broke through the haze of happiness and seduction. Anna wriggled out of his hold, patting Ryan on the chest.

"Sorry, handsome, looks like your plans to have me naked will have to wait. Dog needs come first."

Anna walked away, calling Samson to the back door. Ryan watched her go, admiring the seductive sway of her hips that was all the more attractive given that he knew it was not done on purpose. She was just naturally sensual and beautiful. In that moment, Ryan realized everything about the evening had felt so right. Even this—their passion being interrupted by a dog—felt more normal, and more perfect than anything he'd ever experienced before. He loved how they effortlessly swung from sex and desire, to laughter and teasing. How seamless it was to be a couple at work, around their friends, and here at home.

With a start, Ryan realized he hadn't been to his own apartment, to do more than grab clean clothes, in weeks. Almost every night had been spent together at Anna's, and they had settled into a comfortable routine. Domesticity had never appealed to him, but somehow, he found himself enjoying every minute of it. Cooking meals together, folding laundry, and seeing her lace panties in with his boxer briefs, all of it felt so right. When Ryan thought of home, he no longer pictured his bachelor pad, he pictured this little house, with Anna and Samson.

* * *

Samson bounded back into the kitchen, stopping at Ryan's feet to wag his tail in delight at seeing one of his favorite humans. Anna smiled as she watched her sexy man crouch down to love on the scruffy dog. She tried to figure out exactly when she had started to think of Ryan as 'her man' but saying it—even just in her thoughts—felt good. A sense of peace drifted over her heart and for a brief moment she let herself imagine what life would be like without the specter of Tim hovering in the background of her mind. How it would feel to simply be with Ryan, be in this new life and embrace it without fear. *Maybe he won't try to find me...*Just as soon as the thought crossed her mind, she shook her head to dismiss it. She'd have to be crazy to ever believe Tim would leave her alone, especially if he ever realized what she knew.

Taking a deep breath, Anna tried to force away her ugly memories, to focus again on the adorable scene in front of her. Samson was now laying on his back, with his tongue hanging out as Ryan rubbed his belly. Ryan was laughing softly, and Anna realized only a brief moment had passed with her lost in her thoughts.

Determined to bring back the seductive mood from their drive home, Anna slowly started to unbutton her soft denim shirt, revealing her tight white tank top. She pulled her tank top over her head, before Ryan realized what she was doing. When he glanced up, his eyes burned with instant desire at the sight of Anna standing there, wearing nothing but her jeans and a pale pink bra. Without a word, she started to unbutton her jeans, never losing connection with Ryan's gaze. He slowly stood up and prowled over to her. Running his hands down her arms, his large hands covered her own where they hovered over the zipper of her jeans. The heat radiating off his body caused a shiver of arousal in Anna as he took over and swiftly undid her jeans and pulled them down. He crouched in front of her, lightly grazing the front of her legs with his fingers, softly but purposefully. He helped her step out of her jeans, then gently guided her back a step until she felt the edge of the kitchen counter behind her back.

The silence between them was electric. No words were necessary to convey Ryan's intention when he lifted Anna up so she could sit on the edge of the counter. When he dropped to his knees and pressed a hot, open-mouthed kiss to the front of her damp panties, she gasped. Her chest thrust forward as her head dropped back and Ryan reached up to cup her lace covered breasts with his hands. Wanting him to move things along and find bare skin, Anna tried to reach down between her legs to pull her panties off, but he stopped her.

Ryan stood up between her legs, his erection straining against the fabric of his jeans. He pulled his shirt off over his head, revealing his tanned, muscular torso. The dance of his muscles sent a fresh wave of liquid heat straight to Anna's core, and she squirmed where she sat, desperately searching for relief. He placed one hand on her hip, while the other reached up to undo her bra. Her breasts bounced free, and she shrugged off the straps, drinking in his intense gaze that burned her up from the inside out. When Ryan leaned down and captured one breast in his mouth, loving it with his tongue as his fingers gently squeezed the other nipple, Anna could no longer stay silent. Her breath came out in a moan at the sensations flooding her body. His denim clad erection pressed against her wet core, as he tempted and teased her breasts. She held his head tightly, her fingers knotted in his hair as her legs came up to wrap around his waist.

After what felt like an eternity of torment, Ryan lifted his hands up to cover hers, and gently untangled them from his hair. With a searing glance, and no warning at all, he reached down and took the edge of her panties in his hands before tearing them off.

She had to admit, this take-charge side of Ryan brought their love making to a new level of erotic passion. Despite his intensity, and the lack of romantic words, she felt safe and cherished in a seductive way that was earth shattering. It was all too easy to let go, allow him to take control and dominate her body with his attention.

Kneeling down once more, Ryan lifted her legs over his

shoulders. He didn't waste another second before diving into her wet mound with his mouth. His tongue worked her from top to bottom before he took her clit in his mouth and sucked gently. Anna's gasps and moans seemed to fuel him on as he brought his fingers in to touch her, sliding in and out of her channel, gently at first, before speeding up into a frenzy.

Just when she was certain that she would never survive an orgasm of the magnitude she knew she was in for, Ryan slowed down his pace, bringing her back from the brink of release. She groaned in response, simultaneously welcoming the break in sensation, but also desperate to climb to the peak once more. He didn't disappoint, when he curled his fingers around slightly, hitting a new angle inside of her molten core. In a heartbeat, she was flying high, keening, moaning, and eventually screaming his name as he latched on to her clit again, sucking as he teased her on the inside.

With one final cry, Anna let go, feeling her release wash over her like a tidal wave.

Several moments later Anna became aware of her surroundings, of the hot hulking man leaning on his side next to her. She could sense his fingers stroking her from hip to shoulder, and when she opened her eyes, she could see his lazy, satisfied grin.

"Damn, I'm good."

The triumph in his cocky tone made her laugh. "Oh my god. No you're not, you're terrible. And amazing. And ridiculous. And incredible. And—"

Whatever else Anna was about to say was muffled by his mouth covering hers. She giggled into their kiss, wrapping her hands around his neck. With no warning at all, Ryan picked her up and carried her quickly up the stairs to her bedroom. He lay her down gently on the bed then climbed on beside her.

"You could have stopped at incredible, sweetheart," Ryan said with a wink, as he held his muscular body over hers. His teasing expression turned serious as he stared down at her with such intensity Anna felt as if his eyes alone could set her on fire. "Because that's what you are, incredible."

"I need you, Ryan. I need to feel all of you." Anna didn't care how pleading she sounded, she was so consumed with desire and emotions that she was not ready to face.

Ryan didn't waste a single moment, leaning down to cover her neck and breasts in soft kisses as his fingers danced around her core. He spread her moisture around, making her soft and slippery. Then he flipped onto his back, pulling Anna on top of him. She lifted herself up, sensually touching her body as he quickly rolled on a condom. She slid down on top of his rigid shaft with a groan. The stretching sensation of him filling her deepest channel completed her in a way she never realized she needed.

"Oh fuck, yes."

Ryan's voice was a low rumble as he slowly started to thrust his hips up. Anna quickly followed his rhythm, undulating her body to ride his cock. His large hands grabbed her hips, holding her so tightly she briefly wondered if he would leave a mark, before realizing she wanted him to. She wanted to be claimed by him in every possible way.

Anna leaned forward, letting her long hair fall around their faces like a curtain. She was aching to feel his lips sear her soul. With her hands on his chest, his muscles bunching beneath her touch, she nipped at his lower lip before he growled and caught her mouth in a kiss that stole her breath away.

"This is heaven, Anna. Absolute heaven."

The wonder and passion behind Ryan's words resounded in Anna's heart. As he reached up to kiss her again, he moved them once more so that Anna's back was pressed against the mattress. Their bodies were slick with sweat and arousal as they moved in that timeless dance of passion. He thrust in and out, hitting all the corners of her core. Slowly, but incessantly, she felt the tingle of an impending orgasm build up her spine.

Ryan groaned, and sped up his movements. Anna clutched his shoulders, wanting to fly over the edge with him.

"Don't stop, Ryan... Yes! There... Oh god! Yes!" The last word came out as a scream, as Ryan roared his release and collapsed on top of her.

Hearts pounding in unison, they lay together, Ryan's weight pressing Anna into the mattress. She let out a small sound of protest when he shifted off her to go and deal with the condom. He returned quickly, and lay back down on the bed, pulling her in to his side. She tangled her leg over on top of his, finding her favorite pillow on his chest. With a sleepy sigh, Anna quickly started to drift into sleep. The last thing she remembered before sleep took over was a soft kiss being pressed to her hair, and a nervously hopeful voice whispering quietly.

"I think I'm falling in love with you, Anna."

* * *

The next morning, after a fitful sleep, Ryan was awake way too early. Anna was wrapped around his body, her soft snores telling him that she was still fast asleep. He lay there in the silence, thinking about last night. He hadn't planned to say those words, they had just slipped out. But he meant them—every word. Ryan struggled to decide if he was relieved that Anna was probably asleep by the time he said he was falling in love with her, and likely hadn't heard, or disappointed that she hadn't been awake to say it back to him. If she even would! Now that was a path he didn't want to go down. *What if she doesn't feel the same way,* he worried. No, he was pretty damn certain she was feeling just as strongly for him, as he was for her. The trust, the comfort, the passion between them. A person just couldn't fake that.

Breathing deeply, Ryan pulled his arms even tighter around Anna's shoulders. She shifted in her sleep, letting out a soft hum of contentment. He closed his eyes, and let his conscious mind slip into a daydream. He could see himself in the future, walking hand in hand with Anna. Samson was bounding on ahead of them, chasing after a small child. Now that was a crazy thought. Ryan had never in his life thought of himself as parent material, but with someone like Anna, someone kind, loving, and patient. Maybe being a dad wouldn't be such a terrible idea.

Lost in his thoughts Ryan didn't notice Anna waking up until she slid her lithe body all the way on top of him. He opened his eyes to see her smiling sleepily down at him before she pressed a kiss to the tip of his nose.

He rumbled a low laugh at the adorable gesture. "Well now. That's a damn fine sight to see. You draped over me like a blanket, and the most beautiful smile on your face. I could get used to that."

A nervous look came over her face, as she tugged her lower lip in between her teeth. Her voice was hesitant, but hopeful when she stuttered, "Well, maybe getting used to it wouldn't be so hard? You're here a lot anyway, so I was thinking, do you maybe want to...”

She sat up suddenly, bringing her sex directly over his hardening cock. Somehow Ryan knew she didn’t notice that, as her face grew serious and, adorably, more nervous. Trying to appear unaffected by their position, Ryan folded his arms behind his head.

“God, why is this so hard to say?”

“There’s nothing you could tell me that I don’t want to hear, sweetheart. Just say it. Do I want to... I guarantee the answer is yes.” Ryan’s teasing was rewarded by a laugh from his sweet woman.

“Doyouwanttohaveakeytomyhouse?” Anna said quickly, before looking down, and drawing idle circles on his chest with her finger.

Ryan sensed the importance of what she was asking. This was more than just a key. This was about Anna placing her trust in him, letting him into her home and her life. He knew she was still scared about her past catching up, and he knew he should be more concerned about why that was. This moment, however, was about seeing her take control of her happiness, and the realization that she felt confident and secure in their relationship, made his heart swell.

“I’d love a key, Anna.” His voice was solemn, and he hoped she could see how genuinely touched he was by her offer. Her answering smile was all he needed to see, before he surged upward, pulling her into his embrace with a passionate kiss. As she rubbed against his body, he let out a guttural moan. She responded by shifting slightly and reaching her hand down to grasp his cock. Slowly, Anna worked him with her hand, never letting their lips come apart.

Ryan could feel his arousal building quickly under Anna’s

touch. She affected him in every possible way, making his heart yearn for more. Then, like a bucket of ice water being dumped over his head, Ryan was jolted out of the moment by his deep-seated doubts. Who was he to deserve her trust and love? What did he possibly have to offer in return? What if he turned out just like his father, how could he live with himself if he ever hurt Anna the way his dad had hurt his mom?

Ryan broke free from their kiss with a groan. He needed some space to figure himself out, even if leaving Anna was the last thing he wanted to do. He pushed her hands away, ignoring the hurt look on her face. Climbing out of bed, he avoided her gaze as he searched the floor for his clothes. "Sorry, Anna, I forgot, I need to meet Jake for inventory. I'll call you later, okay?"

He pressed a fast kiss to her face before walking out of the bedroom, leaving her still wrapped in her sheets. He felt like a total asshole walking out on her like this, but knew that if he tried to explain, he would only hurt her more by confiding his fears and indecision. No, leaving her now was the right choice. He just hoped she would understand later.

After a quick, cold shower at home, Ryan wrapped a towel around his waist and headed to his closet to get some clean clothes. His mind was still full of confusing emotions. On the drive home from Anna's house, the commitment apparent in her offer, combined with his whispered admission of love struck him with the force of a semi-truck. How the hell did it get this far? Ryan Carlisle, falling in love and accepting a key to a woman's home.

He sank down onto his bed, still dripping from his shower. Absentmindedly he tugged the towel tighter, rubbing the tops of his legs. *What the fuck am I doing? I can't hurt her.* No, he would never hurt Anna. Would he? Ryan wanted desperately to believe he would never hurt the one woman who had come to mean more to him than anyone else outside of his own family and Jake. But could he ever guarantee that? The weight of his past, his father's mistakes all came crashing down onto his heart. Ryan had lived with the fear of turning out like his dad for so long, it was a heavy load to try and shake off. Still, if ever there was a woman who deserved the best of what Ryan could offer, it was Anna. She could be the woman to chase away his demons, if Ryan could only trust in himself to let her.

16

Chapter 15

Several hours later, Ryan found himself sweating in the storage room of The Lucky Strike, as he and Jake completed their weekly inventory. He was so consumed by his conflicting emotions from the previous twenty-four hours, he didn't notice Jake's mounting frustration until his voice pierced his thoughts.

"Dude, what the fuck is wrong with you! That's the third time you've put a case of Frog River in the wrong spot," Jake cried.

Ryan jolted into awareness at the exasperation in his friend's voice. "Shit. I'm sorry." He quickly moved the offending keg into its correct position before slumping down to sit on the floor.

Jake's face morphed from frustrated to concerned in a heartbeat. He sat down beside Ryan, turned to his friend, and asked, "What's going on man?"

Ryan sighed, and leaned his head back so he could stare at the ceiling. He still hadn't fully processed his thoughts, and now the layer of guilt over how he had left Anna this morning rested on top of his chaotic feelings of self-doubt.

"Anna offered me a key. A fucking key. I've never had a key to a woman's place before, hell I've never been to a woman's place as many times as I have to hers. We even do our laundry together, dude, laundry. My boxers are mixed in with her thongs. It's domestic. I love it and I'm terrified of it." Ryan paused, breathing heavily at the force of his confession. After a moment he continued, "I'm falling in love with her, Jake. It's only been a few weeks, but you know this is the longest committed relationship I've ever had. I find myself imagining the rest of my life with her, but at the same time, I can't shake this feeling that I'm not cut out for forever."

Jake looked thoughtfully at Ryan for a moment before he responded, "First of all, get your head out of your ass. You are being a moron, Ry, and I say that with love. Longest relationship? Bullshit. You and I have been friends for over a decade. You have known Callie for almost a year. You're committed to us, you care about us, right? No, you aren't doing our laundry, because that would just be creepy. But we see you all the time, and you have never let us down. So why would Anna be any different?" Jake slugged him in the shoulder, then crossed his arms on top of his knees and spoke the words that Ryan so desperately wanted to believe. "When are you going to realize, you are not your dad. I know you won't cheat on her, you're not going to leave, and you would never hurt her on purpose. That's not who you are. Look, I get that it's scary. Trusting yourself and trusting someone else is fucking terrifying. But it is so goddamn worth it."

Jake paused and Ryan could feel the weight and solemnity of his words slowly sink in. However, the urge to disagree, to not believe his friend, was still strong.

"I know you're right, Jake, but—"

"I wasn't finished," Jake interrupted. "Love is like bungee jumping. Scary, exhilarating, life changing. You're about to jump off the ledge, and Anna is your rope. You just need to trust the rope."

Silence stretched between them as Ryan absorbed all that Jake was implying. Maybe the root of his fears went farther than just his similarities to his dad. *Maybe I don't trust anyone not to hurt me, just as much as I don't trust myself not to hurt them.* With that sobering thought hanging in the front of his mind, Ryan pushed himself to his feet.

"Thanks, Jake. I hear where you're coming from."

Jake followed slowly, looking closely at Ryan, gauging his reaction. "You hear me, but do you believe me?"

Ryan finally met Jake's gaze and nodded. "Yeah, I'm starting to. She's worth it man, I'll do whatever it takes to keep her happy."

"Then you had better apologize for whatever you did or said when she offered you that key. Because I'm guessing you freaked out and did something stupid." Jake clapped Ryan on the back, before hefting a box of liquor bottles into his arms and heading toward the front of the bar. As he walked away, he stopped and turned. "I can finish up here. Go and find your woman and make this right."

Ryan grinned at Jake's retreating back. Somehow Jake knew just how to cut through the bullshit in Ryan's head, and get him to see the truth.

* * *

Anna folded one of Ryan's shirts that had been in her laundry.

The soft feel of the cotton knit was comforting, as was the basic act of putting his clothes in a drawer next to hers. She had been on autopilot all morning since Ryan had left, going through her daily tasks like a robot, unaware of the world around her.

Anna was not a stupid woman. She might have made some bad decisions in her past and turned a blind eye to her ex's behavior for far too long, but she was no idiot. She knew that Ryan's abrupt departure had little to do with inventory at the bar, and a lot to do with his heart.

She refused to allow herself to feel hurt or embarrassed by the fact that he had bolted just moments after she offered him a key to her home. No, Anna knew that Ryan was battling his own demons. She recalled something Callie had said to her weeks ago.

"Ryan's dad was a real jerk. Treated his mom like garbage and walked out on them when Ryan was just a kid. From what Jake says, Ryan looks exactly like him. I think he's always been worried he'll turn out like his dad if he allows himself to get close to someone."

Anna sighed as she considered the past twenty-four hours from Ryan's perspective, using Callie's observations. She could understand why he had bolted right after making the commitment to having a key to her home. Knowing the type of male role model he had as a boy growing up, of course he was scared of commitment. From what she had seen over the last several weeks, she knew he was a kind and generous man, and that hurting someone, even inadvertently, would destroy him. How could she get him to see that she trusted him, fully, and had no fears of him breaking her heart. If anything, Anna worried that she would be the one to cause pain in their relationship. There was no way of knowing what Tim might attempt or when.

Every moment they spent together, Anna battled with the guilt that she was placing him and their friends in harm's way.

Anna wandered into the kitchen, stopped beside Samson's bed and sat down on the floor with him. He lifted his head and rested it in her lap with a snuffle of contentment. She took a deep breath, allowing the peaceful love of an innocent animal wash over her.

"What are we going to do about that man, Samson?" she mused aloud, figuring the dog was as good a listener as anyone. "I'm falling in love with him. So how do I get him to realize he is perfect just the way he is, and I would trust him with my heart and my life?"

"I'd say those words will work pretty damn well, sweetheart." Ryan's deep voice held a tender note.

Anna jumped in surprise. "What are you doing here? I didn't hear the door open. Oh god, that was not how I wanted to tell you!" She moaned in embarrassment. The realization that Ryan had just overheard her profess her love for him, to the dog, was mortifying.

He laughed then sat down beside her on the floor and wrapped his arm around her shoulder. "The door was unlocked, Anna," he chided her gently. "I guess you and Samson were having such a serious conversation you didn't hear me come in." He tightened his hold around her shoulders, and when he spoke again, his voice was soft, hesitant but hopeful. "Did you mean it? Are you really falling in love with me?"

Anna turned in his arms so she could look him in the eyes. What she saw there melted her. Love was brimming on the surface of his clear blue eyes, infusing his face with a joyful, peaceful look.

"Of course I meant it, you silly man. Do you think I would lie to the dog?" she teased, trying to keep the conversation light as she fought her own nerves. Would he say it back?

"Thank god for your honesty, woman. Because I am most definitely in love with you, and your confessor of a dog."

Relief and love flooded through Anna's body as she scrambled to climb into Ryan's lap. She needed to feel him beneath her, within her, around her.

"I. Love. You." Anna interspersed her words with kisses that she peppered all over Ryan's cheeks. It may have only been a few hours since they were naked in her bed, but she was consumed with need for him.

Ryan stood up swiftly, pulling her up with him. He bent and placed one arm under her knees, and lifted her into his arms, and strode determinedly toward the bedroom.

"Anna, you need to be naked and I need to be inside of you, now. When I'm done, you'll feel my love so deep in your soul you'll never forget."

17

Chapter 16

The euphoric bliss of admitting their love for one another carried Anna and Ryan through the following week. Jake had begun to tease Ryan for what he called the "lovesick fool" look on his face. Ryan had taken the ribbing, knowing he had been just as annoying when Jake first fell for Callie. Besides, his heart was so full of love, there was no room for something as petty as frustration or anger. Not toward his best friend.

One afternoon, Ryan brought Anna to have coffee with his mother. Molly Carlisle was just as taken with Anna as Ryan figured she would be. The two women talked for hours about every topic under the sun, from Anna's dream to become a teacher, to Ryan's childhood antics. Pure happiness filled his soul seeing the two women he loved more than anything, getting along so well. When they stood up to put on their coats to leave, Ryan glanced at his mother to see her looking wistfully at the two of them. When she noticed him watching, she smiled warmly, and reached her hands out to clasp each of theirs.

"Anna, words cannot express how happy I am right now. You have brought my boy to life in a way I never thought possible. I see your heart and his wrapped around each other, and it warms my own. You are always welcome here, my dear, and I hope Ryan brings you around again soon."

Anna leaned forward and gave her a hug. "Thank you, Molly, you have raised an incredible man, and I feel lucky to have him, and now you, in my life." She turned to Ryan with a wink. "I'll definitely be back soon, let me know when you find the photo album of baby pictures!"

Molly and Anna laughed as Ryan rolled his eyes at that. "Okay, let's get out of here before Mom thinks of any more ways to embarrass me."

With a final flurry of hugs, they left. As Ryan held open the door of the truck for Anna to climb in, she paused with one foot stepped up into the cab and turned to him.

"Your mom is incredible. It's clear that she is where you get your amazing heart from. Thank you for taking me to meet her, I hope you never lose sight of how lucky you are to have her."

Ryan knew her poignant words reflected her pain over losing her parents and her aunt. He leaned into the cab of the truck to press a kiss to her forehead. He didn't know how to ease her grief, or if he even could.

"I know how lucky I am. I'm sorry I will never get to meet your parents, or your aunt. But, trust me, Mom considers you family now. I know it's not the same but..." his voice trailed off, as he stood there, uncertain of what to say.

Anna smiled softly, and when he looked closely, he was relieved not to see pain in her eyes. Her voice was strong and sure when she said, "It's not the same, but it is pretty wonderful. I can't wait to spend more time with your mother." A wicked glint came to her expression. "Especially if she shows me naked baby pictures..."

Ryan groaned. "Damnit, not the baby pictures, I was a weird looking baby."

"I'm sure you were absolutely adorable," Anna said.

"Let's just hope that if we ever have kids, they take after their mom, not their dad."

As soon as the words left his mouth, Ryan winced. *Too soon you idiot, too soon,* he thought to himself as he watched Anna for her reaction. When she just laughed, oblivious to his embarrassment, he breathed a sigh of relief.

* * *

Anna shivered at the thought of having children with Ryan. She had laughed when he made the comment about what their kids would look like, but that laugh was just to cover up the hope and the worry that battled in her heart. The allure of imagining a family of their own, filled with love and happiness, was so strong.

When they pulled into the parking lot at the pub, instead of rushing to climb out, Anna and Ryan sat quietly together. Absorbing the emotions that swirled between them.

Anna was silent, as she thought about how lucky he was to have so many people in his life who loved him. An intense wave of grief hit her, as she realized she had no more family. Who would pull her out of the darkness if she had to leave Ryan?

"You're lucky, Ryan, you have friends who are like family and a family who adore you," she blurted out as she brushed a tear away that had slipped down her cheek. "Please promise me you will never lose sight of what a blessing that is."

"Oh, sweetheart, I won't, and you have them now too. You

know that, right?"

Anna's breath caught on a sob as Ryan gathered her in his arms. She cried, tears of love, tears of sadness. Grief from losing her parents, Aunt Theresa, her life in Portland, it all finally flowed out of her. Deep beneath the tears, Anna realized she had never truly allowed herself to feel her sorrow from losing her family. She had been so focused on being strong and keeping herself safe, on breaking free from Tim's control. There, in the parking lot, safe in Ryan's arms, Anna finally felt the walls around that part of her heart break down.

She was vaguely aware that Ryan was whispering words of love as he comforted her, words she couldn't comprehend, but could feel the caring emotion behind. Eventually her river of tears slowed and came to a stop. Lifting her head from Ryan's shoulder, Anna was startled to see the time on the clock in the truck.

"Oh my god, I'm so sorry, we're late for work!"

"It's totally fine. Jake knows we're here, but that we need some time. Just breathe, Anna."

Anna sagged back into his arms. "I can't believe that all just came out of me. What a mess."

Ryan tipped her chin up, so she was forced to look at him. "You are not a mess, Anna. You're beautiful, and strong, and incredibly loving. Most importantly, you are loved. By me, by everyone. Please believe me when I say this. Jake, Callie, Noah, my mom, even Reagan, Melanie, and Chase. I know they all adore you and are here for you no matter what. You're not alone anymore, babe. And you never will be again."

His words rang out in the cab of the truck and infused the air with such love and strength, Anna felt the tears build behind her eyes again. This time, instead of tears of grief they were tears of joy. She had no choice but to believe him, so strong was the conviction behind his statement. She, Anna Thorn, was no longer alone.

A few moments later, after Ryan had finished kissing away any sadness or trace of tears, they emerged from the truck ready for work.

Ryan held her hand tightly as they walked in the back entrance of the pub. Anna could hear music coming from the front near the bar, but when she tried to pull away from Ryan so she could prepare for her waitressing duties, he tugged her into Jake's office. Jake was sitting behind the desk working on his computer. He looked up with a warm smile.

"Everything okay, you guys?"

Ryan answered for them both. "Yeah, sorry we took a while to come in. Look, Anna is going to start behind the bar with me tonight. She can take over serving if it gets too busy but for now, I want her close."

A look passed between the two men. Anna was relieved that once again Ryan had anticipated her needs so easily. After the emotional roller coaster of the day, she wasn't ready to be apart from him either. She knew, and clearly so did he, that the added stress of putting on a smile to serve customers would take more energy than she had that night.

Jake nodded, clearly understanding Ryan's unspoken message.

"No problem. If needed, I can help the servers when Chase goes on. See you guys out there."

The next hour went by smoothly. Anna helped Ryan pour drinks and slowly managed to fully regain control of her emotions. Callie and Reagan came in and sat at the bar, chatting with Anna over a glass of their favorite peach ale. If anyone noticed anything off with her, they didn't mention it.

After filling another drink order, Anna realized they were running low on bottles of Frog River, a crowd favorite—especially with many of the patrons who came to watch Chase perform. With a wave to let Ryan know that she was going to the storage room, she headed down the hall to grab another case. On her way, Anna smiled as she passed one of the waitresses coming out of the washroom. Just before she could open the door to the storage room, a strong hand grabbed her and pushed her out through the back door into the empty parking lot. As she was spun around, Anna smiled expectantly. It had to be Ryan, sneaking a moment of privacy.

Instead, all of her worst fears came true as she looked upon the face of the most evil man she had ever met.

"Tim," she gasped.

18

Chapter 17

He sneered at her. A condescending, cruel look that made it clear he had something horrible in mind. Anna shuddered with fear as she looked at the man she once thought she loved. His slicked-back hair, the designer clothes he wore as a way to show off the riches he had gained by being a kingpin in the seedy world of drug dealing. The cold glint in his eyes was proof that the man had no heart, no soul. She knew without a doubt, he wouldn't hesitate to do whatever he felt necessary to get what he wanted.

"Did you really think you could leave me? You belong to me, Anna Thorn. If you want to live in Portland, fine we'll live in Portland. But make no mistake, you cannot get away from me. When we get home, I will show you what happens when you defy me like this." His voice was chilling.

Anna stumbled backward, her eyes darting around seeing nothing but a parking lot full of cars—no people, everyone already inside enjoying the evening. No one was there to help her. Feeling the tendrils of hopelessness seep into her soul, she could only pray that his being here didn't mean he knew that she had witnessed his act of murder.

"You don't want me, Tim, not anymore. I have no idea how you found me, but—"

"How I found you?" He laughed, an evil laugh that made her feel like a bug he was about to squish with his Italian loafers. "You left the goddamn letter from that lawyer in my house. I finally found it last week, and decided to pay you a visit. Your helpful neighbor, Sally, was all too willing to tell me where you work. I'm surprised, Anna, I thought you would be more careful. You never know who you can trust, now do you." His words were taunting, a cruel reminder that Anna had trusted Tim blindly at first.

Anna cursed her stupidity. In her rush to get away, the letter from Aunt Theresa's lawyer must have fallen from her bag. And of course, it included the address for her Portland house. Before she could think any more about that, or worry if Tim had hurt Sally, he took another menacing step toward her. He was deranged. Did he actually think she would let him stay here, in Portland, with her? Fall back into his trap? Not a chance. Yet her strength wavered under the intensity of his evil power. Anna shuddered at the thought of what her fate may be, especially if he learned of the secret she held. Then again, maybe—just maybe—she could use that information as leverage to get away.

Taking a deep breath, Anna realized he had cornered her against the back wall of the pub. She held her hand in front of her, and, hating the tremble in her voice, she tried desperately to bluff her way into getting him to leave.

"I know what happened, Tim. I know you killed someone that night you took me to your meeting. I saw you do it and I've got video proof. If you let me go, I'll go and get it to give to you, you can destroy the video and I will forget I ever knew you.

But if you don't, my friends inside are going to figure out I'm missing soon, and they know to send the video to the cops."

If only her empty threat was true. Why had she not told Ryan the whole truth of why she was so scared of Tim. Instead, Ryan had no idea that she had the SIM card from her old phone hidden in her house, the only proof of what Tim had done. If she let him take her now, no one would ever know that he was a murderer.

"You dumb bitch." Tim lunged at her, grabbing her arm painfully. She cried out, but he pulled her toward the parked cars. "Blackmail? Really? Goddamnit, Anna, you're stupider than I thought. You'll never be free of me. When I'm done with you, whatever you think you saw, whatever proof you think you have, won't even matter anymore."

Anna screamed as he wrenched her toward him, twisting her arm so hard she felt something snap. Her vision went blurry, the pain so intense she was certain she was going to pass out. This was it, the moment she had feared for so long was here. Tim would take her away, and she would lose everything once again.

* * *

"Here you go man." Ryan pushed the last bottle of Frog River toward the waiting customer. *Where's Anna with the new case?* he wondered to himself, realizing it had been several minutes since she had gone to the back. Spying one of the waitresses at the end of the bar, he called over to her, to see if she knew anything.

"Hey, Veronica, have you seen Anna? She was going to get some more bottles of pilsner, we're all out."

She came over with a confused look on her face. "Sorry, Ryan, I saw her going to the back storeroom about ten minutes ago, but that's it." She paused, thinking, before giving Ryan a worried look that made his heart sink. "I did see some rich dude heading down the hall after her though. I figured he was just going to the bathroom." Veronica glanced quickly around the bar. "But I don't see him here."

He didn't wait to hear what else she would say, Ryan took off running down the hall. He was dimly aware that Jake and Callie had noticed him leave, and hoped that Veronica would fill them in. Deep in his soul he knew Anna was in trouble.

Ryan slammed open the back door of the building just in time to hear Anna scream as the stranger holding her arm twisted it backward.

Ryan charged at the man, knocking him off balance. The element of surprise was with him, and he managed to get in some solid punches before the other man, who Ryan had instantly surmised must be Tim, was able to break away and stand up. Out of the corner of his eye, he saw Callie crouching down by Anna, and Jake advancing slowly to lend his support in the fight. Thank god his friends had figured out something was wrong and had followed him right away. Tim must have seen the odds shift against him as well, because Ryan could see the indecision in his eyes as the evil bastard seemed to hesitate, likely debating his chances of trying to escape.

Ryan and Jake both tackled Tim as he turned to run, taking him down to the ground. Jake pinned him and pulled his hands behind his back. In the distance, sirens wailed. Someone must have called the cops.

Jake looked up at Ryan, a determined and protective glint in his eye. "I've got this bastard, Ry, go and see to Anna."

With a nod of thanks Ryan stood up and turned, running across the pavement to where Anna sat, quietly crying as Callie held her injured arm. Callie looked up with a furious set to her face as Ryan sat down behind Anna and gently pulled her back against his body.

"He broke her fucking arm, Ryan."

Breathing deeply to try and control the anger and adrenaline he could feel coursing through his veins, Ryan looked at Anna. She had turned her head buried her face in his shirt, curling into his body as much as her injured arm would let her.

Suddenly he was paralyzed with the uncertainty of not knowing exactly what else had happened to her. "Anna, baby, are you okay? Can you look at me?"

She peeked up at him with tear-soaked eyes. "I'm okay now you're here. But it hurts, it hurts so much."

"I know, sweetheart, I know."

He leaned down slowly, pressing kiss after kiss all over her face. His arms tightened around her body, and when he felt her relax into his embrace, any doubts or fears that had once lingered in his mind washed away and all Ryan could feel was the strength and beauty of his love for the woman in his arms. He vowed then and there that he would make it his sole duty to ensure that she would never be alone, never be scared again. He murmured into her hair over and over how much he loved her, and that she was safe now. Slowly he felt her sobs slow down.

Ryan didn't move a muscle from his hold on Anna until the police and paramedics arrived. Even then it was difficult for him to let go of her so that the paramedics could get her on the stretcher to assess her injuries. He looked up to see two police officers pull Tim up off the ground and slap handcuffs on him.

He knew Jake would take care of informing the officers of what had happened, at least as much as they knew. Anna would still have to give her statement, but he quietly asked the paramedic who was loading the stretcher into the back of the ambulance if that could wait. Callie was standing next to him and must have overheard his request because she touched his shoulder to get his attention.

"They're taking her to Oakville Memorial. I'll call ahead to my colleagues; I think Mel's on shift. I can try to talk to the cops who will be going there with her, they'll probably recognize me from work. I can ask if they will wait until she's had her arm treated before asking for her statement."

Ryan smiled gratefully at Callie as he climbed into the ambulance beside Anna, who was now drowsy thanks to the pain medication the paramedic had given her.

"Thanks, Cal."

"Take care of our girl."

He nodded firmly. "You know I will."

The ride to the hospital was quiet, save for the beeps of the monitors hooked up to Anna. Ryan held her good hand tightly as he watched her lying on the stretcher. Images, memories flashed through his mind. Hearing her scream, seeing her trapped by Tim. An endless cycle of torment made worse by Ryan's imagination taking over and thinking about what could have happened if he had not been there in time.

Their arrival at Oakville Memorial Hospital was surprisingly uneventful. Two police officers had followed the ambulance and walked in with them. Ryan's glare did nothing to deter them from hovering close by while Melanie examined Anna and assessed her arm. Ryan felt helpless as he stood back, letting the medical team do what they needed to do. When Sandy, a nurse he recognized from the pub as a friend of Callie and Melanie's, wheeled Anna away for an X-ray, Mel pulled Ryan aside.

"She's okay other than the arm, Ry. I don't think it needs surgery so we can just put a cast on it and she should be fine in a few weeks." Mel paused, glancing over at the officers who were still waiting in the corner of the curtained area Anna had been in. "You're going to have to drop the caveman protective boyfriend act, buddy. You can't be in here when they interview her."

Ryan looked at her in shock. "What the hell? I'm not leaving her to do that on her own, Mel, no way."

She looked at him sympathetically. "I know you want to be here for her, but it's procedure. They might let me stay though, if that will help?"

Ryan nodded, running his hands through his hair. "Yeah, I just don't want her to be alone right now."

Mel touched his arm in support. "We'll get her through this, then you can take her home and hold her close."

"I'm not sure I'll ever be able to let her go."

* * *

Anna was exhausted. She was dimly aware it was some ungodly hour in the morning, but she had no true concept of time. It felt as if mere moments had passed since she first saw Tim in the parking lot of the pub, but she knew, logically, it had been hours. Her arm throbbed, despite the pain medication she had been given. The bright lights of the ER were painful to her eyes as she fought to keep them open as one of the police officers took her statement. Reliving what had happened with Tim that night was torture. The fear she felt in the moment that he grabbed her surged to the surface of her memories. Thankfully, as her doctor, Melanie was allowed to stay in the room. Her hand on Anna's shoulder helped her to stay in the present moment and not get lost in the memory of the trauma she had suffered.

After Anna finished giving her statement, she knew the officer was still speaking, but she was no longer paying attention. Fear was steadily building inside her, thoughts of what could have happened if Ryan and Jake hadn't been there threatened to overtake her conscious mind with panic. She needed Ryan. His arms around her, his heart beating strongly, those were the only things that would make her feel safe. She didn't tell the officer about what Tim had done back in California. Maybe she should have, but there was no way she was telling that story without Ryan holding her tightly.

"So, given the obvious nature of your injury, as well as the witness statements, Mr. Fox will likely be held on felony charges awaiting trial. If there's anything else you can tell us about him, here's the phone number for the precinct."

Anna realized the police officer was holding out a business card. She took it numbly, and nodded, pretending she had heard everything he said.

Thankfully, Melanie stepped in when Anna was unable to formulate a response.

"Thank you, Officer, but if you're finished, my patient needs to go home and rest now."

"Of course, Doctor Haynes, we're done here. Miss Thorn, you take care. And call us if you think of anything to add."

Anna nodded. After the police officer left, Ryan came striding back in, and she sagged back against her pillows in relief. She cursed how weak she felt, how desperately she needed him, but when he gathered her in his arms Anna felt herself take the first deep breath she had in hours.

"Take me home, Ryan, please."

19

Chapter 18

At some point on the drive home from the hospital, Anna fell asleep. The crash from the adrenaline of the previous night's events, combined with the sedating medications she had been given hit hard. So hard that even when Ryan lifted her out of the truck and carried her inside, she barely stirred. He was thankful for small mercies, knowing that sleep was likely the most important medicine for Anna right now.

The house was eerily quiet, as Samson had already been picked up by Jake and Callie earlier. Anna's jacket, still at the pub, held her keys, making it possible for them to collect the dog.

Ryan carried Anna upstairs and laid her down on the bed before easing off her shoes. He considered trying to undress her to make her more comfortable but chose not to for fear of waking her up. Instead he propped up her broken arm on a pillow, stripped down to his boxers and climbed into the bed on the other side of Anna. As he gently pulled her close, he simply lay there for a while, watching her. His heart was filled with gratitude for her safety, anger that she had been hurt, and guilt that he had not been fast enough to prevent Tim from ever touching her. His heart heavy with the turmoil of emotion, Ryan eventually fell asleep.

Screaming woke him up, fear leaping into his throat, bitter tasting and vile. Anna bolted upright, panting heavily as her hands fought off an invisible attack.

"NO! TIM, NO! STOP! HELP! RYAN!"

Ryan threw the covers off, and grabbed her hands, trying to slow her motions. "Sweetheart, you're okay! I'm here. You're safe." Tears began to fall down his face as he looked at the woman he loved, held captive by her terror.

"Baby, you're safe. Please wake up, Anna. I love you," Ryan pleaded with the semi-conscious Anna, as he stroked her uninjured arm and she slowly came to full consciousness.

"Ryan? Oh my god, Ryan, I was so scared." Anna sobbed as she collapsed into his embrace. He continued to hold her and murmur comforting sounds as he tried to force his own heart to stop racing.

After moments that felt like hours, Anna's breathing settled. Ryan wondered if she had fallen back to sleep, but her quiet voice spoke into the darkness.

"I'm never going to be free of him. He'll always be there, if not in person then in my mind. He wants to kill me; I know he does."

Ryan was silent as he pulled her even closer, as if his embrace could fend off every threat. How he wished it were that simple, that he could slay her dragons and promise her safety forever. What if the justice system failed them? What if Tim were to be released on bail? Ryan had a sinking suspicion that there was more to Anna's history with Tim than what she had told him, but unless she let him in, how could he keep her safe.

"I swear to you I'll do whatever it takes to keep you safe." Ryan kissed the top of Anna's head, knowing his words were empty promises in the face of such evil. "Baby, this might be hard to talk about, but I need to know the whole story. I need to know what we're up against. You said Tim was into some bad shit back in Sacramento, but why won't he leave you alone? Why do you think he'll try to kill you?"

Filled with dread, Ryan remembered a conversation he had with Callie back when he was just getting to know Anna. Torn between desperately not wanting to know the answer, and understanding that he had to hear the full truth, he asked, "Anna... did he... did he ever hurt you? Physically I mean?"

* * *

Deep down Anna had known she couldn't hide forever from the truth of what she knew. The memories of that bitter night in December were always there, buried deep inside her mind. Still, she hesitated. Would Ryan be mad that she had not told him everything sooner? Maybe what happened could have been prevented, if only Anna had not been too scared to come forward.

Sitting up again, she gently disentangled herself from Ryan's arms, immediately missing the warmth she found there. Her hands twisted in her lap as she tried to gather her thoughts and figure out how to start.

With a deep, cleansing breath in and out, she looked at Ryan, taking in the concern and love etched on his face. She caressed his cheek, trying to ease the lines of worry forming on his forehead.

"No, Ryan, he never hurt me like that. He was a high-level drug dealer, but he never hit me."

Ryan's sigh of relief brought a sad smile to her face as she continued, "It's worse than that. He didn't hurt me physically, just emotionally. The reason he wants to kill me is because he... Oh god, I don't know how to say this. I never said anything to you, or to anyone, because I was desperate to forget what happened." Anna's voice broke at the daunting task of reliving her darkest memory.

"Anna, you can tell me anything. You know I love you, and I'll be here for you no matter what."

Ryan spoke softly, but there was a thread of steel in his words. That strength was there to protect Anna, shield her from whatever nightmare was to come. When he took her hands, the warmth of his grip emphasized how ice-cold Anna's were. She smiled softly again. He always knew what to say to bring her comfort.

"I know you do, Ry. Just, please, let me get this out, okay?"

"I will, but you have to let me hold you. I need to hold you and feel you close to me," he replied.

Anna nodded, and snuggled back into his embrace. Truthfully, it would be easier to talk without seeing his face.

"One night, Tim took me with him for one of his 'client meetings' as he called them. More like a sketchy drug deal done in a secluded alley. I still don't know why he made me come out with him that night in particular. I suspect it's because he knew I wanted to leave him, so he didn't want to leave me at home alone. By this time, I had already begun to think about how to get out of the relationship. My aunt had died, and the letter from her lawyer had arrived just a few days earlier. I still have no idea how the lawyer found me, but thank god he did.

When I saw that I had inherited her house, it felt like a sign. This was my way out."

Anna was glad Ryan couldn't see her face, as she knew he would see the raging emotions at war inside of her. Getting the full story out into the open was her only priority, and if Ryan tried to interrupt her, even if only to provide comfort or reassurance, she knew she would crack and not be able to finish.

"Something in me told me to record what happened in that alley. Maybe it was Aunt Theresa's angel guiding me, who knows. But I did—I pulled out my phone and recorded the whole thing. I couldn't hear what was said, but I saw what happened. All of it."

Taking a deep, calming breath in and out, Anna closed her eyes, and, for the first time, allowed the images from that night to resurface.

"At first, all I could see out of the back window was Tim talking with a man. They were behind the car, and Tim's back was to me. Then suddenly, I guess something went wrong, Tim pulled a gun. Where he had been hiding it, I don't know. I had no clue he even had any guns, which might have been stupidly naïve of me, but there you go. A second later, Tim shot the other man, twice. I couldn't see any blood or anything, but that sound, and then seeing the man drop to the ground, I'll never forget that." Anna shivered, as the sound of those gunshots rang in her mind. "Then, Tim just stood over the body, staring at him for a moment, before making a phone call. I guess he was calling someone to come and deal with the body. After that, he got back in the car and drove us home without saying a word."

Ryan had not made a sound, nor moved a muscle, throughout Anna's story. When her voice trailed off, her only confirmation that he had heard everything was a slight tightening of his arms around her.

The air was charged with emotion. Anna felt as if an immense weight had been lifted from her heart just by finally sharing her burden of memory. At the same time, she was filled with trepidation. What would Ryan say, how would he react, knowing that she had witnessed a murder, and done nothing?

Ryan pulled away from Anna, turned so he was sitting across from her and looked straight into her eyes. She drank in the serious set to his face, somber yet filled with love.

Slowly, he said, “Anna, I can’t even begin to understand what you went through. You have to be the strongest, most courageous woman I have ever met, to have lived in that hell and to have successfully left.” He took her hands, his thumbs gently stroking the backs of them as he continued, “Did he know that you saw what happened? That you recorded it?”

Anna shook her head. “No, I don’t think he knew I saw what happened, until last night when I told him. That’s why I think he wants me dead.”

Surprise flitted across Ryan’s face when Anna admitted she had told Tim that she knew what he had done.

“Why the hell did you tell him?”

She shrugged. “I thought maybe I could use it as blackmail. I don’t know why, Ryan. It was stupid. I know I should have taken it to the police in the first place, but I was just so scared. I had this ridiculous hope that he would just leave me alone and I could forget it ever happened. Of course, all the hope in the world couldn’t erase the fear I’ve lived with ever since that night. The fear that he would come and find me. And that is exactly what happened isn’t it. Damn, I’m a moron.”

Anna dropped her head into her hands as the realization hit her. Maybe all of this could have been prevented if she had just taken the video to the police right away. Back then her focus had been on getting out of Sacramento and as far away from Tim as she could. How foolish she had been to think he wouldn't try to find her.

Ryan gently tipped her head back up, then leaned in and pressed a sweet kiss to her lips. He held her hands again, this time folding them together in Anna's lap in a way that his large, warm hands covered hers in a cocoon of support.

"Anna, stop beating yourself up. You made the best decision you could at the time. You focused on your safety, which makes a hell of a lot of sense to me. And, that decision landed you here with me. Now we can go to the police together, you can show them the video, and hopefully that will lock Tim away for a very long time." He lifted their hands so he could press a kiss to her knuckles. "And I will be there beside you every step of the way. You escaped him on your own, now let me be there with you when you close the door on that part of your life. Hopefully forever."

Anna nodded, fresh tears pooling in her eyes. But this time, they weren't tears of fear or sadness, they were tears of love. She knew without a doubt that Ryan meant every word, and that he would do everything in his power to support and protect her.

"Okay, I'll tell them everything."

20

Chapter 19

Later that morning, after finally going back to sleep for a couple more hours, Anna and Ryan found themselves parked outside the downtown precinct for the Portland Police Department. Anna's heart pounded so loudly she was certain Ryan could hear it. The thought that Tim was just a few feet away, although thankfully locked in a cell, still filled her with trepidation.

"You don't think I'll have to see him, do you?" She turned to Ryan nervously, as her stomach took a nosedive at the idea of seeing Tim again.

"Not if I have anything to say about it," Ryan said.

Anna smiled at him gratefully. "You can't go in there acting all *macho protector,* Ry, they might not even let you stay in the room with me when I give my statement."

Ryan looked at her somberly. "I know, but please tell me you know that I will fight as hard as possible to be by your side every step of the way."

Touching his cheek lovingly, Anna felt her heart grow impossibly full as she looked at the man who had shown her what true love and respect was. This was a man who would walk through fire for her.

"I know you would, and I love you for that. So very much. But I can do this, Ryan. As long as I know you are in the building with me, and that you'll hold me when it's over, I have the strength to do this."

Ryan pulled her back into his arms, infusing her with that very strength she needed. "Then let's get this over with, sweetheart. So I can take you home and show you just how amazed I am at your courage." He climbed down from the truck and walked over to help Anna down, carefully supporting her injured arm. Together they walked into the precinct, and at the front desk, asked to speak with the detective in charge of the case.

Moments later, they were shown into a sparse office, with a desk and two chairs that faced a windowless wall. An older man sat behind the desk peering down at some papers. When the desk sergeant introduced Ryan and Anna, the detective stood up and shook their hands before he invited them to sit down.

"I'm Detective Ronson, thanks for coming down Miss Thorn. I assume this is something you feel comfortable speaking about in front of your friend here?"

Anna nodded rapidly. "Absolutely, Detective, in fact, I would feel more at ease if he stayed—if that's alright of course." She glanced at Ryan nervously. "I'm not sure what the rules are though. Is that okay?"

Detective Ronson smiled kindly at her, easing her nerves. "Of course it is. I want you to know, we take domestic violence cases very seriously. With multiple witnesses to what Mr. Fox did to you last night, your physical injuries, as well as your statement about your previous relationship with him, we have enough to hit him with felony charges." He paused, his brow wrinkling as he studied Anna carefully. His scrutiny was thorough, but

Anna could tell it was not accusatory.

"Unless that is, you have something to add, Miss Thorn?"

Anna sat up straighter in her chair, grateful Ryan was right beside her, his hand gently rubbing circles on her back. She could feel the heat from his palm radiating through her, infusing her with the courage and confidence to share her story one more time.

"Please, Detective Ronson, call me Anna. And yes, I do have more to add."

Glancing at Ryan, she took in his nod and smile of support, then turned back to the detective. With a deep breath, she began.

"A few months ago, Tim took me with him for one of his meetings..."

* * *

Hearing the story a second time in less than twenty-four hours didn't lessen the impact for Ryan. His gut clenched hearing Anna repeat the horrific events of that night in California. He knew how hard it must be for her to relive everything that she saw, and his heart ached with wanting to take away her pain, take away her fear.

He noticed Detective Ronson was paying rapt attention to every word and chose to take that as a good sign that he was taking Anna seriously. She handed over her phone, where she had inserted the SIM card she had removed from her phone in California.

"The video is saved on the SIM card. I took it out of my old phone and brought that with me when I left California."

Detective Ronson didn't reply, as he was absorbed in watching the video over and over, studying it closely. Eventually, he looked up at Anna, an indescribable look on his face.

"Anna, I need to call my colleagues down in Sacramento. Would you please wait here for a moment?" Without another word of explanation, he pushed back from his desk and strode out of the office, taking Anna's phone with him.

Anna turned to Ryan, worry etched on her face. "What is going on, Ry? Why does he have to call Sacramento PD? Doesn't he believe me?"

Ryan was just as confused as Anna, but instantly tried to reassure her. "Of course he does, that video is proof that what you said you saw is what really happened. I'm sure he just needs to check with them about something..." Ryan trailed off, realizing he also had no clue what was going on.

Thankfully Detective Ronson returned quickly, before Ryan had to come up with any more excuses for his abrupt departure. He sat back down in front of them, and handed Anna her phone with the back plate removed, where she could see the SIM card had been removed again.

"I'm sorry, Miss Thorn, I mean Anna, but we need to keep the SIM card for evidence." He folded his hands on his desk, leaning forward slightly. The energy in the room grew even more weighted. As Detective Ronson opened his mouth to continue, Ryan reached over and grabbed Anna's hand, needing the connection and knowing instinctively that she did as well.

"When we ran Mr. Fox through the system, we determined that he is a wanted felon. The process is underway to transfer him down to California to face multiple charges of drug trafficking. Where this gets interesting is, Timothy Fox has been evading police and hiding underground for the last few months. Interestingly, the date of his disappearance from the narcotics scene coincided with the death of an undercover Drug Enforcement Agency officer in the Sacramento area. The DEA has been working closely with the Sacramento PD, and they strongly suspected Mr. Fox was the perpetrator. Your video confirms the evidence we had of the location of the murder, thus proving he did in fact pull the trigger on the agent. The DEA has had agents searching California looking for him and thanks to you, Miss Thorn, we've got him sitting in our cells."

When the detective finished his jaw-dropping statement, he sat back in his chair and with a satisfied smile on his face, he folded his hands in his lap. "Please make no mistake. I am very sorry you were injured last night. However, that incident brought the subject of a DEA manhunt straight into custody. He killed an officer of the law, Miss Thorn. That's a capital offense in many states and a lifetime imprisonment in others. So, let me be the first to assure you, he will never see the light of freedom again."

Stunned, Ryan turned to Anna to see her frozen, in an equally shocked state. That was not at all the news that he was expecting to hear. Sensing that she was still trying to get her reaction under control, Ryan spoke up. "Thank you for telling us that, Detective Ronson. I hope you can understand that it is quite a shock for Anna to hear all of this. Do you need anything else from her? Or can I take her home now?"

Detective Ronson nodded understandingly. "Yes, it is heavy news to try and process. I want to thank you both for coming down here today." The detective stood and reached out his hand to give them his business card. "That will be all we need from you for now, I suggest you go home and rest. If you have any questions about the case, please don't hesitate to reach out." He paused, and looked thoughtfully. "And, Anna, if you are able to remember any names of known associates of Mr. Fox, or anything else, give me a call. We certainly have enough to lock him up for his lifetime, but if we can take down some of his associates in the narcotics ring that would be even better."

Anna nodded, still sitting ramrod straight in her chair. Ryan ached to fold her into his arms and feel her soften into his embrace. He would do anything to erase the tension that radiated off her right now. He stood, and gently tugged Anna to stand, keeping a tight hold of her hand. Silently, they walked through the station, murmured goodbye to Detective Ronson at the door, and headed out to his truck.

It worried him that Anna didn't say a word the entire drive back to her house, but he kept his own feelings at bay, to give her space after the bombshell that had just dropped in their laps.

They pulled into her driveway, Ryan killed the engine, and turned to her. Her expression was one of emotional exhaustion, mixed with undeniable need.

"Take me inside, Ryan, take me to bed. I need you to make me feel whole again. Right now, I'm just so empty. Facing the fact that Tim was a cop killer, has taken everything out of me. I need you to fill me up," she said, her voice quiet but clear.

Ryan searched her face, uncertain if she truly meant what she was saying. "Sweetheart, are you sure?"

"Yes, Ryan, you are the only thing that has made me feel safe these past few months." She looked at him, her eyes pleading. "Please, Ryan, I need to be in your arms. I need your love, your strength. I need you."

"You've always got me."

* * *

The relief Anna felt at surrendering to Ryan in that moment was everything she desperately needed. She knew he would carry her, care for her, and love her both physically and emotionally. But right now, she meant what she had said. The emptiness she felt inside was not necessarily a bad thing. Talking to Detective Ronson had removed a weight from her soul that had taken up so much emotional space, that now she was left with a void that she wanted to fill with love and happiness.

Just as she had hoped he would, Ryan opened her car door and lifted her easily into his arms. She snuggled in and pressed a kiss to the side of his neck as he carried her into the house. It was only when they were inside that she suddenly realized that with all of the trauma she had been through, she had not thought about her dog once in the last twenty-four hours.

"Samson! Ryan, where is Samson?"

"It's okay, sweetheart, he's with Jake and Callie. They picked him up yesterday. Samson is fine."

She relaxed back into his arms with a deep sigh. "Oh, thank god. You really thought of everything. Thank you."

Ryan's arms held her strongly as he gazed down at her. She could feel the heat of his stare and looked up at him. His expression was full of admiration, so intense she had to ask, "What is that look for, Ry? You look like I cured cancer or something."

Ryan chuckled, as she had hoped he would. The mood was far too serious, and she needed him to help make it lighter.

"Anna, your selflessness amazes me. You've been through hell and then some, and you're worried about the dog. I just think it's incredible how you always put others first, even a pet."

Anna smiled, warmed by his compliment. "Samson is more than just a pet you know, he's my tie to my Aunt Theresa. He's important. But, thank you. Now, can we please go upstairs so you can show me just how amazing I am?"

Ryan's deep laugh carried them upstairs and straight into the bathroom. He set her down then turned on the hot water taps for the bathtub. Once she realized his intention, Anna wrapped her good arm around his waist, stood on her tiptoes and whispered in his ear, "I hope you're going to join me in there."

The heated stare he gave her was answer enough, but the rough tone of his voice and his sexy words was enough to send shivers of lust straight to her core.

"You bet I am. We'll get clean, then we'll get dirty," he rumbled. Slowly he helped her remove her shirt, taking care over her cast. "We'll take extra care of that arm. Can't get it wet, babe." His care and attention softened her heart even more. Anna knew she would never find another love as true as this.

When she stood before him naked, she didn't miss the way his eyes roamed her body appreciatively. Wanting to see him, Anna reached for his shirt, fumbling when her injured arm stopped her from stripping it off him. Letting out a frustrated growl, she was rewarded when Ryan pulled it over his head one handed, in that sexy way men did. He quickly discarded his pants, climbed into the tub and held out his hand for her to help her in.

She settled back, leaned against his rock-hard chest, and let the hot water lap over their naked bodies. Ryan made no move to seduce her at first. He seemed just as content as she was to simply be together in that intimate moment. Steam swirled around them, aromatic with the bath oil Ryan had added when the water was still running. The silence was broken only by soft splashes against the side of the tub when they shifted their bodies even slightly.

As she relaxed into the warmth of Ryan's body, Anna was pleasantly surprised by how comfortable it was to rest her injured arm on the edge of the tub. Ryan's hands worked across the top of her shoulders, gently kneading away the tension. His hands slowly roamed over her collarbone, drifting across the tops of her breasts. He moved under her arms to help support her cast, wrapping his large hands around her torso until his fingers found her nipples just under the surface of the water. She sighed appreciatively when he started to play with her breasts, gently tugging and teasing her. Anna tipped her head back, opening herself up to his mouth. He didn't disappoint her, as he bent down to press open kisses across the smooth column of her neck and shoulder.

A sharp tweak of her nipple elicited a gasp, and then a moan, when one of Ryan's hands slid further down her body. He stroked up and down her torso and teased her by pausing just at the top of her sex, barely grazing her before bringing his nimble fingers back up to play with her breasts.

"Ryan..." She sighed softly. He responded by turning her face and kissing her, filling her with the depths of his love and passion.

Caught up in his kiss, Anna didn't notice his hands leave her breasts until she suddenly felt his touch between her legs, as he slowly separated her slick folds. His fingers found her clit, and started to tease it, stirring up an inferno of heat inside her core. Still his touch remained gentle and caring. She felt cherished, loved, and protected.

When Ryan slipped one, then two, fingers into her tight channel a moan escaped between her lips.

"That's it sweetheart, feel me loving you."

His guttural voice betrayed the control Anna could feel in his taut muscles. She felt so connected to him, that she could tell he was focused solely on her pleasure, no matter the strength of his own desires. Ryan continued to play with her clit and slide in and out of her core, as he found the spots to apply just the right amount of pressure. Anna quickly felt her orgasm build, knowing instinctively that her release would come hard and fast, and likely only take the edge off her need. She wouldn't feel whole until all of Ryan was inside her, caressing her and loving her as deeply as only he could.

Seconds later her instincts were proven right when Anna skyrocketed toward her climax. As she lay in Ryan's arms, she slowly felt her heart rate return to normal, before she turned to face him, careful not to splash water on her cast.

"I love what you do to me, Ryan, but I need all of you," she looked at her arm and grimaced, "and I don't think that will work in the tub right now."

Swiftly but cautiously, Ryan climbed out of the tub and quickly wrapped a towel around his waist. He reached down and lifted Anna out with ease. He tenderly toweled her dry, before lifting her into his arms again.

"You know I can walk, right?" she teased, secretly loving his strength and the way he couldn't seem to stop carrying her everywhere.

"Yeah, I know you can. But why should you, when I can take care of you like this." His matter of fact response was enhanced by the adoring look on his face.

Gently Ryan set Anna down on the bed, where she moved to

the head and settled down under the duvet. She watched as he finished drying his own body, admiring the ripple of muscle across his chest as he twisted to reach his legs. When he was done, he tossed the towel into the bathroom, then climbed onto the bed beside Anna. She welcomed his embrace as he came over on top of her body. His hands framed her face and his legs gently eased hers apart as he settled. She gave herself over to whatever pleasure he would bring, knowing that with Ryan she was safe and loved.

"I love you, Ryan." The simple statement was not nearly enough to convey the depth of her emotion, but those four words came straight from her heart.

"I love you too, Anna. With everything I am, I love you."

Ryan's heartfelt response was the match that ignited the inferno of passion between them. Anna reached her head up to capture his lips in a kiss. As their tongues wove together, Ryan kept one hand up beside Anna's head as he slid his other hand down her body, lifted her leg and wrapped it around his body. They pressed closer and closer together, their bodies melted into one. Anna rubbed her wet core along Ryan's rigid shaft, eliciting a groan from him, a deep, erotic sound that she felt zap straight down her spine.

Ryan stretched his arm to grab a condom from the bedside table, and quickly rolled one on, never losing contact with Anna's mouth. She slid her hand down to wrap around his covered cock, feeling it throb with desire. She guided it to her hot entrance, and slid the tip up and down, until it was covered in her essence.

"You're killing me," Ryan ground out the words as Anna continued to torture them both.

She smiled at him before shifting her hips just enough that

he could slide all the way home. They both let out a groan of pleasure when he sank deep into her. This was what Anna needed. This feeling of completeness, as if her soul had found its way home, wrapped in Ryan's love. Slowly he began to rock his hips forward and back and slid his cock along Anna's inner walls, creating delicious friction. She felt their connection in every inch of his body that touched hers, and deeper—in the air between them as their energy and emotion combined into a perfect dance of love. Anna lifted her hips to meet him thrust for thrust, as they locked their lips together, sharing breath and taking in each other's passion.

Anna could sense her orgasm barrelling down on her with the speed and intensity of a freight train. Anxious to have Ryan fly off the edge with her, she clawed at his back with her good hand, cursing that she couldn't hold him tightly with both arms. He must have sensed her building desperation, because Ryan suddenly leaned back, never losing his connection to her core. Sitting back on his heels he pulled Anna upright so that she straddled his legs. Now she could wrap her arms around him, as he held her tightly.

"Oh god, Ryan, that's... you... oh yes!"

The new angle gave such power to her arousal, Anna was certain she would climax right then, but somehow managed to hold off as Ryan continued to thrust into her over and over.

"Fuck, Anna, I'm so close. This feels so goddamn good."

His rough words showed Ryan's loss of control, as he leaned down and captured her breast in his mouth. He sucked deeply at her nipple, as Anna shrieked in ecstasy at the mixture of sensation. The gentle tug of erotic pain at her breast, combined with the heat and fullness at her core. When he released her nipple, and leaned his forehead down to touch hers, Anna knew what was coming.

"Let go. Fly, sweetheart, and I'll fly with you."

With a final moan of pleasure, Anna cascaded into an orgasm so full of emotion, so full of deep passionate love, she was certain she would burst from the sensation. When Ryan roared into his release right after her, they collapsed back onto the bed, with his cock still inside her.

It was several moments before either of them could speak or move. When Anna was at last able to lift her head from Ryan's sweat-covered chest, she looked at him, love shining in her eyes.

"Thank you for taking care of me, thank you for protecting me, thank you for loving me."

Ryan lifted his head up to kiss her lips before responding. "I can't imagine my life without you in it, Anna. Thank you for letting me love you."

Anna smiled down at the man she adored with all her heart. Suddenly she knew what she wanted more than anything else.

"I don't want to live my life without you. Move in with me, Ryan. Let's spend every day and every night loving each other."

"Yes."

Without saying another word, Ryan rolled her over onto her back, and showed her with his body over and over again just how good an idea he thought that was.

21

Chapter 20

Several weeks later, Anna's arm was nearly healed. She had an appointment with her doctor to remove the cast in a few days and that day couldn't come soon enough. Ryan had been her dedicated caregiver, as he helped her in the shower, cooked for her, and spoiled her so much with affection she was sometimes overwhelmed with his love.

Moving Ryan into her home had been a seamless transition. Ryan's few meaningful belongings fit in easily thanks to all the space in Anna's house. Now it was more than just a drawer in the bedroom that held some of his clothes, he had a section of the closet, multiple drawers, and even space in the front closet for his gym gear.

Slowly they settled into a comfortable routine, living a life together that was not bound so strongly by fear and worry. Anna helped at the bar when she could but, with one arm still in a cast, she was limited in what she could do. So, Jake and Ryan had finally decided to hire a manager for the pub. Thankfully, Noah had stepped into the role, claiming it would be temporary, until he found a new career path for himself. It was going so well with him helping, that Jake, Ryan, Callie and Anna were trying to convince him to make it a permanent decision.

Even with all the happiness and peace in her life, Anna still felt unsettled. She knew Tim could no longer hurt her, not now, and hopefully not ever. Yet somehow, him being in the county prison just over the border in northern California while he awaited trial was too close for comfort. He was not eligible for bail, so Anna knew she should feel safe, but she couldn't seem to shake the feeling that there was more drama to come.

She had begun seeing a counselor, who was helping her work through the trauma, and find ways to reclaim her confidence and courage. The counselor had made a huge difference for Anna, as she developed tools and strategies to manage her fears and reactions. One night, long after the pub had closed, Anna and Ryan lay in bed, entangled in each other's arms. Laying in the dark was the place that Anna felt the safest telling Ryan her innermost thoughts, and where she would often talk to him about her therapy sessions.

"I just wish I knew what it would take for me to be ready to take my life back. In therapy today, Sandy was telling me I need to give it time. That someday I would wake up and feel like myself again. I do feel like myself, I'm just still so anxious all the time. It feels as if I have had so many wonderful things happen lately, I can't help but worry, what if my good luck runs out..." Anna's voice trailed off to a whisper.

Ryan's arms strengthened their hold around her. "Sweetheart, it is completely understandable that you would still feel nervous. However, I think Sandy is right and that it's going to take time to trust that you are safe. You can't rush that." He propped himself up on his elbow to look her in the eyes. Even in the dark, she could feel their connection humming between their gazes. "So, you listen to me, Anna Thorn. Your luck is not going to run out. You have been through hell and came through it with courage and a smile. If there is anyone who deserves the best happiness and love-filled life possible, it's you. And I'm going to be right here beside you no matter what. Got it?"

Anna lovingly reached a hand up to caress Ryan's cheek, easing the fierce lines that came over his face every time he went into what she had affectionately dubbed his "protector mode."

"Okay, big guy, I got it. And I love you, so very much. Thank you for always knowing just what to say."

"I'm just doing my job as the luckiest boyfriend in the world." Ryan leaned down and pressed a soft kiss to Anna's lips.

As happened every time their lips met, the spark of lust turned into an inferno. With a moan Anna pulled Ryan down on top of her, deepening their embrace. Her foot slowly slid up his leg until she could wrap it around his hips, just below his firm ass. She could feel his cock nestled in between her legs, hardening against her sex with every passing moment. Ryan let one hand trail down her body until his questing fingers reached her throbbing center.

"Goddamn it, Anna, you're so ready for me, aren't you, babe," he growled.

Anna moaned as he deftly slid his fingers around her entrance, teasing her. "Please, Ryan, just... make me feel... you."

Ryan lifted his head, to smile wickedly at Anna. "You just stay right there. You'll feel me, all of me, as I love all of you."

Then he slid down her body until his shoulders were wedged between her legs. Slowly he pressed open kisses to her inner thighs, slowly dragging his mouth higher and higher until he was at her center. He clutched her hips and loved her with his tongue, sliding his fingers in and out of her drenched core. Anna writhed underneath his touch, gasping and moaning as he worked her up to the ultimate peak of desire.

The sensations building within them both went deeper than lust, stronger than passion. This was no ordinary love, this was a captivating, powerful force that felt more than love—if such a thing were possible.

With a scream of Ryan's name, Anna let her orgasm flood her senses. Spine-tingling heat zapping through her body, she collapsed onto the bed as he drew out her release with every warm swipe of his tongue. When she stopped shuddering, he slowly moved up the bed and pulled her into his arms. She quickly fell asleep entwined in his embrace. No more words were needed, Anna was safe in his arms.

* * *

Ryan poured a mug of hot coffee, added in Anna's preferred vanilla syrup and placed it on the tray next to the plate filled with her favorite breakfast foods. He'd woken up early and decided he was going to treat her to breakfast in bed. When he crawled from the warmth of their bed earlier, he had gazed down at Anna, who was still peacefully asleep. Not a moment passed that Ryan didn't feel eternally grateful that she had come into his life. Somehow this beautiful woman had burst through his defenses and shown him a part of his heart he never knew existed. Ryan couldn't imagine ever loving anyone as much as he loved Anna. He was not a religious type, but Ryan often found himself praying to the universe that she could find her inner peace. It tore him up when he saw the shadows cross her face, and knew she was thinking of that asshole awaiting his trial in prison. He despaired wondering if she would ever be free of that demon.

As Ryan picked up the tray, he heard Anna's phone ring. He could hear her soft, sleepy voice mumble hello as he wandered down the hall, curious to see who was calling so early.

The pale, shocked look on Anna's face when he entered the bedroom clenched his heart with fear. He quickly put the tray down on the dresser, climbed onto the bed, and pulled her into the safety of his arms. He couldn't hear the other person on the phone, but Anna's soft gasps of surprise, murmurs of understanding, and whispered "thank you for telling me" had his heart pounding. Without realizing he tightened his hold around her, desperate to protect her from whatever was happening.

Anna hung up the phone and stared silently down at the duvet as she picked at invisible lint for a moment. It nearly killed Ryan not to say something, to demand she tell him what had happened, but instinctively he knew she needed a minute to process.

When she finally spoke, her words were a shock, but also a cathartic release of tension he hadn't realized he had been carrying.

"He's dead. Tim is dead." Anna finally looked up, tears spilling from her shining eyes. "It's over, Ryan, I'm finally free."

Ryan was speechless as the impact of her words sunk in. He pressed a kiss to the top of her head, trying to formulate his response.

But before he could say anything, Anna continued, "That was Detective Ronson. He got a call from the warden at the county prison where Tim was being held to wait for his trial. Apparently, he was in a fight last night. They suspect it was someone from a rival drug ring. Tim was stabbed and taken to the infirmary, but he didn't survive." Anna pulled away and turned to look at Ryan. Hope warred with guilt in her eyes as she asked, "Am I a horrible person to feel so happy he's gone?"

At that Ryan found his voice. "God, no, sweetheart. You are not a horrible person and you are also not the only person thankful that he is finally out of our lives, forever. He deserved whatever happened to him, and I for one, want to shake the hand of the scumbag who stabbed him. Little does he know, he did us a massive favor."

Anna laughed through her tears at that, and Ryan was gratified to see the smile emerging on her face.

"You're right. We should send him a thank you note."

Ryan snorted at that, before pulling her back into his arms. Settling against the headboard, they lay snuggled together. Something about this moment felt different. As if this were finally the moment their lives together could truly begin. His sentimental feelings were echoed by Anna's words.

"All I feel is relief. Well, relief and excitement for our future. Together. Being with you has been the biggest blessing in my life, and I know that whatever else happens, making it through the last few months has made us stronger. You have made me stronger. I love you, Ryan, so much."

Anna twisted in his arms and cradled his face gently in her hands as she pressed a sweet kiss to his lips. When they separated, Ryan was seized with the desire to say something that he knew would forever change their lives.

"Marry me, Anna."

Anna looked equal parts shocked and excited by those three

words. Ryan realized he was probably doing it all wrong, and that she deserved a far more romantic proposal than this, but he couldn't help himself. He climbed out of bed and went down on one knee on the floor beside her.

"I don't have a ring; I haven't planned any of this. But as you just said, we are stronger together. This is our beginning, Anna, the beginning of forever. I want nothing more than to have you by my side for every moment of it."

Anna threw back the duvet and leapt off the bed into his arms. She peppered his cheeks and neck with kisses, as he laughed and held her close.

"Can you give me the words, babe? I think I know what your answer will be, but a guy needs to hear the words at a moment like this."

"YES! Oh my god, yes, Ryan. Of course I will marry you. I love you so much. This is perfect. You are perfect. We are perfect." Anna punctuated her statements with more kisses, as they tumbled to the floor.

Samson came running in at the commotion and barked as he danced around them. Laughing, Ryan reached up to scratch the dog behind the ears, before turning back to the beautiful woman in his arms.

"I used to think perfect was overrated. That love and commitment were not for me. You have changed all that, sweetheart. You're right, we are perfect. Now get back in that bed and let me show you just how perfect our love is... And then, we are going shopping for a ring."

* * *

Standing in the jewelry store, hand in hand with Ryan as they looked at engagement rings, Anna took a moment to reflect on how her life had changed. Was it really only a few months ago that she was living a life of fear with Tim, feeling hopeless about her life, and too scared to make a change?

Her aunt's passing was still a source of sadness in Anna's heart. She wished she had come home in time to see Aunt Theresa again. Yet Anna knew that if there were such a thing as guardian angels, Aunt Theresa was hers.

Anna was suddenly drawn to a beautiful ring in the corner of one case. It had a pear-shaped diamond, with small sapphires on either side. Sapphires were Aunt Theresa's favorite stone, and Anna could remember her wearing a pear-shaped sapphire ring almost every day. This felt like one more sign from her aunt that everything would be okay.

Looking at Ryan, she felt the love of her aunt shining down on her as she drank in the sight of the man who had brought so much to peace and happiness to her life. She knew her aunt would approve, of the man and the ring.

When Ryan slid the diamond and sapphire ring onto her finger, it was an exact fit. Just as the two of them were the right fit for each other.

"It's perfect."

Epilogue

"Promise me you'll make another one of these when Ryan and I get married? Please?" Anna's voice was filled with awe as she watched Reagan adjust the beautiful wedding cake made of three tiers of heart-shaped brownies. Each tier held a different flavor, and was decorated with edible flowers giving it a rustic and delicious appearance.

Before she answered, Reagan took a step back, placed her hands on her curvaceous hips and examined the display with a critical eye. When she seemed satisfied with her work, Reagan dusted her hands together and turned to Anna with a smile.

"Of course I will. As much as I hate to admit it, because I know I bitched about how much work was involved, this was a lot of fun to create."

The two women had become fast friends over the last few months as they helped Callie plan her special day. As maid of honor and bridesmaid, they had formed a strong bond. Reagan's brownies now filled Anna and Ryan's freezer as often as they did Callie and Jake's.

Anna rubbed her hands together in delight. "Excellent. I'm going to go and find that hunky fiancé of mine and tell him you said yes!" She walked away with a little wave to Reagan, on a mission to find the man who had made her dreams come true.

When Anna caught up to Ryan, he was chatting with Noah. With a quick apology to his brother, she took Ryan's hand

and pulled him out into the hallway, desperate for a private moment.

She found a quiet alcove with a padded bench and tugged Ryan over to sit down. He pulled her into his lap before leaning down and kissing her deeply. "Hey, sweetheart, are you getting some good ideas for our wedding?"

"Our wedding." She sighed, happy to be in his arms again. "I can't believe I'm planning our wedding. I honestly never thought this day would happen."

"Well it's happening, Anna. As soon as you will let me, I am going to make you my wife." Ryan's eyes held a possessive heat as he looked at her lovingly.

She shivered at his words, consumed with desire. Would she ever stop wanting him? Probably not.

"I can't wait to be Mrs. Carlisle."

With a low growl, Ryan captured her lips in another kiss infused with the passion that constantly simmered between them. They stayed locked in each other's arms for several more moments, until the sound of Jake's father announcing it was time for speeches pulled them from their reverie. Smiling, laughing, arm in arm, they walked back into the main reception room. Once Anna was in her seat, Ryan made his way up to the podium to give his speech. Anna watched him go, admiring the way his body filled out his suit. She was certain she would enjoy seeing that suit on the hotel room floor later that evening, even more than seeing it on his muscular body right now.

After the speeches were over, Anna grabbed Reagan's arm as the other woman walked out of the bathroom.

"There you are! It's time for the wedding party to dance together while Chase sings the song he wrote for Callie and Jake. Let's go, this might be the only time I let you put your hands on my man." Anna winked. If Ryan had not been the best man, and Reagan the maid of honor, there was no way she would have been able to tear herself away from dancing with him all night. But, for the sake of tradition they would.

Reagan groaned. "That's exactly what I need right now. Dancing in uncomfortable shoes and listening to Chase McCormick sing a love song."

Anna knew her friend was attracted to Chase. Heck, everyone knew, maybe even Chase himself. She was sympathetic to Reagan, knowing how uncomfortable it would be for her being front and center on the dance floor while Chase performed. Still, Ryan had told her that he and Jake suspected Chase had feelings of his own he was hiding. Maybe tonight would be the push the two of them needed.

* * *

Ryan walked up to Anna and Reagan, marveling at the beauty that shone from his fiancée, as he did every time he saw her. He pressed a kiss to the top of Anna's head, then he took Reagan's hand and escorted her out onto the dance floor where Jake and Callie waited.

"Hello, Miss Maid of Honor, how lovely to see you. Looking especially beautiful might I add."

"Thanks, Ry, you're looking pretty dashing yourself. That suit must be giving Anna a good preview for your own wedding day."

Ryan chuckled. "Yeah, my girl is loving it." He spun her out and back in, as Chase's crooning voice sang in the background. Over Reagan's shoulder, he could see Chase on stage. His hands cupped the microphone gently, his eyes were closed, and the man's talent came through as he poured his soul into the lyrics he sang.

"And I knew that someday

I would find you

My everything

My one truth..."

Reagan sighed wistfully, and Ryan shook his head at her with a gentle smile.

"Reags, I say this with love. Stop being so shy and go for it."

Reagan stopped dancing, dropped her arms to her side and stood there, frozen until Ryan lightly nudged her back into movement.

"What the heck are you talking about, Ryan Carlisle?"

Ryan rolled his eyes at her, before nodding towards the stage as Chase finished his song. "Trust me, woman, anyone with two eyes can see how you two are circling each other. He wants you, you want him, so just go for it already."

Now it was Reagan's turn to scoff. "You're crazy. He doesn't want me. And I don't..."

"Don't lie, Reagan."

"Fine, you got me. I think he's hot as hell. But there's no way he would have any interest in me."

"Whatever you say." Ryan smirked, seeing the perfect opportunity to force his two friends to work their shit out. He spun Reagan out into a twirl once more, this time letting go at the end.

Chase was there and caught her easily in his arms. Ryan watched the two of them fall into step, Reagan with a dazed look on her face and Chase smiling triumphantly.

"What did you do, babe?" Anna walked up and tucked her

arm around his waist.

"Hopefully, set it up for those two to open their eyes to each other."

* * *

Reagan wobbled on her heels and was about to curse at Ryan when two strong hands wrapped around her waist, and the low voice that had consumed her dreams for months murmured in her ear.

"Easy there, I've got you."

The feel of his hands on her body burned through her dress like a brand on her skin. Reagan looked up, into the deep eyes that had been the subject of many late-night fantasies.

"Chase."

"Reagan. So, I'm hot as hell, am I?"

Reagan backed away out of his arms, flushed with embarrassment. "Oh my god, you heard that?"

Chase grinned, then reached out and tugged her back towards him. He placed her hand on his shoulder, before clasping her other hand against his chest.

"Sure did. I'm flattered. And wondering why the hell this feels like the first time we've said more than two words to each other."

Reagan rolled her eyes. "Oh please, you're probably drunk and feeling the romance in the air. I'm the closest single woman and now you know I'm attracted to you, so I'm an easy target..."

Chase stopped moving and fixed her with a glare that was so hot, Reagan wilted under the intensity.

"Reagan Grant. Let me correct those ridiculous things you

just said. Number one, I'm not drunk. Haven't had a drop. Number two, you're right, this is romantic. Number three and five can all be ignored because I'm glad you're single but I sure as hell don't see you as an easy target. Which leaves Number four. You're attracted to me. Well guess what, Red, I'm attracted to you too. Have been for a while, and that sexy dress you are wearing has been driving me crazy all night. I can't stay away from you any longer, and the longer you are in my arms the more of an idiot I feel for keeping my distance all this time."

She must have died and gone to heaven. That was the only explanation for the fuzzy warmth Reagan felt spreading through her body as she absorbed Chase's words.

No, this was real life, and Chase was leaning down towards her, looking like he was going to kiss her. This couldn't be happening. The man of her dreams was claiming he was attracted to her, and she didn't know how to handle it. Decades of low self-esteem and multiple painful relationships with shallow, judgmental men sent Reagan into a tailspin. The pull she felt towards Chase, the sexual attraction, all of that could only mean one thing. Any relationship between them, would surely end in heartbreak for Reagan.

His lips brushed hers, softly, tentatively. He was giving her control to deepen their embrace. Her rational mind saw this and admired it. Unfortunately, panic took over. She broke off their kiss and pushed him back.

"I can't do this!"

She backed away, feeling a crack in her heart at the confused look on Chase's face.

Then Reagan Grant turned and ran.

* * *

Want more Lucky Strike Lovers, including an EXCLUSIVE bonus scene from Jake and Callie's wedding day? Sign up for my newsletter by visiting www.authorjuliajarrett.com

What To Read Next

The entire Lucky Strike Lovers Quartet is coming to Amazon and Kindle Unlimited soon!

Loving Callie - Available now

Protecting Anna - Available now

Serenading Reagan - Coming soon

Romancing Melanie - Coming soon

About the Author

Julia Jarrett is a busy mother of two boys, a happy wife to her real-life book boyfriend and the owner of a rescue dog from Guatemala. She lives on the West Coast of Canada and when she isn't writing contemporary romance novels full of relatable heroines and swoon-worthy heroes, she loves to run, practice yoga, drink wine and read.

You can connect with me on:

https://www.authorjuliajarrett.com

https://www.facebook.com/juliajarrettauthor

https://www.instagram.com/juliajarrett.com